Old Money

LINCOLN MACVEAGH

Tower House Books
New York

TOWER HOUSE BOOKS
4304 Newtown Road, New York 11103

Copyright © 2012 by Lincoln MacVeagh

ISBN: 978-0-9858948-0-1

www.towerhousebooks.com

Printed in the United States of America
1   3   5   7   9   10   8   6   4   2

Old Money

1

The Avenue Club sits on the west side of Park Avenue between 53rd and 54th Street. It is large, it takes up almost half a city block, but to the average passerby it's easy to miss. There is no sign on the door, no emblem on the awning, and there are no snarling gargoyles on the grey limestone façade to catch your eye. The club was designed in the 1870's on the model of an Italian palazzo, and the man who designed it was later murdered by his mistress on a platform at Grand Central Station, but none of that romance is visible in the architecture. In fact, the only thing that makes the building remarkable is that it still exists.

Stop for a moment on the sidewalk nearby and look up. You'll notice the club is dwarfed by giant glass office towers on all sides, and that tells you something important. Because while it takes money to build a skyscraper in midtown, it takes a lot more money to resist building one, and so far the Avenue has resisted for over a hundred and thirty years. What else in New York can boast such longevity?

On a warm spring afternoon Wallace "Puff" Penfield passed under the club's navy blue awning and pushed his way through its revolving door. Puff Penfield was the President of the Avenue Club, and in his opinion, it was the best private club in New York. It was older than the Century, friendlier than the Brook, richer than the Metropolitan, and unlike the University Club, it wasn't choc-a-bloc with women and foreigners. At the Avenue it wasn't enough to be successful, you had to be the right sort of person, and that, Puff believed, was how it should be.

"Hello Freddie," said Puff amiably.

"Good afternoon Mr. Penfield, sir."

Freddie was the doorman at the club and he'd been sitting behind the same mahogany desk since before Puff's father died more than twenty years ago. Just at the moment Freddie was flipping through the real estate listings in the *Daily News*, mulling over the purchase of an apartment for his daughter who had recently graduated from City College.

"What's your opinion of the real estate market, Mr. Penfield? I'm considering a junior four in the Bronx."

"Always worth looking at. There's good value in the Bronx and the great thing about buying an apartment, even if the market goes down, you can still live in it." Puff smiled inwardly. It pleased him to talk real estate with Freddie; it was one of the things he loved most about the Avenue.

Puff was an awkward man in many respects. He was ill at ease with his social inferiors, and outside the club he wouldn't have known how to speak to someone like Freddie. But inside the club Puff could talk to anyone, and he especially prided himself on his relations with the staff. He knew all their names, and he knew all their wives' names; and although he understood there was a distinction between members and employees, in his heart he felt they were all part of the same family. Blinded by affection, he confused the pleasure of swimming in the club pool with the privilege of cleaning it.

Puff now started walking up the wide staircase (he never took the elevator) toward the changing room on the fourth floor. He ran into various members on their way down, and he greeted each one by name:

"John."

"Puff."

"Henry."

"Puff."

"Baxter."

"Puff."

Each of these exchanges was accompanied by a quick nod of the head, and taken together they reflected one of the club's strongest traditions. It was the tradition of courtesy. At the Avenue, members did not pass in the hall without greeting each other by name.

"Hello Puff. How's Trixie?"

"Well thanks, Peter."

Puff climbed past the smoking room and the walk in humidor where the members kept their cigars; he climbed past the Pratt Room where club functions were held; past the dining room and the bar and the library; past the billiards room with its extraordinary brass spittoons reaching up to your waist; and when finally he reached the fourth floor, he stopped halfway along the corridor to poke his head into the club's little barber shop.

"Hello, Mr. Penfield," said Carlos cheerfully.

"Good afternoon, Carlos. I'll be with you right after I get a little exercise. Have my chit ready."

If you've never heard of a chit, a chit is a little piece of paper and it's how everything at the Avenue Club gets paid for. Because another of the club's great traditions was that no money should change hands within its walls. Cash was useless. Haircuts, drinks, and poker debts were all paid for by chit, and if anyone wanted to leave a Christmas tip for Freddie or Carlos, he signed a chit for that, too.

Puff entered the dressing room and walked over to his locker. It wasn't a locker per se, but rather a decent sized cubicle, complete with hooks, hangars and a cushioned bench to sit on. Each cubicle had a curtain, for those who wanted privacy, but Puff never closed his curtain because it was considered bad form. The dressing room was a social place. It was more like a lounge than anything else, and in addition to the changing cubicles that lined the walls, there were armchairs and sofas scattered throughout. There was even a collection of small dining tables where the members could eat lunch.

The great benefit of eating lunch in the dressing room was that you got to eat naked. At the Avenue, the freedom of nudity was highly prized, and standing in front of his locker, Puff was completely surrounded by male flesh. To his left, an old banker was discussing portfolio management while rubbing ointment on his bare backside; to his right, a young lawyer scanned the pages of the *Wall Street Journal* with hairy balls hanging off the edge of his chair; and directly in front of Puff, Tweedle Barnes lay dozing on a green leather sofa with nothing but a small towel loosely covering his privates.

"Hello Tweedle," said Puff. "How's my Ball Bearer?"

Tweedle was the club Ball Bearer. It was an honorary position which meant that he carried the ballot box (which was stuffed with marbles, hence balls) from the admissions committee to the President's office on election nights, and it earned him a free bottle of scotch twice a year.

Tweedle snorted awake and rubbed his face.

Tweedle spent most of his afternoons alternately reading and napping in the club dressing room. He was an elderly man, in his seventies, and he had a handsome face, a patrician's voice and a marvelous head of silver hair that he wore neatly parted to one side. Tweedle had been a member for as long as anyone could remember, but he was nonetheless an oddity at the club. No one knew much about him. Some people said he was a failed poet and others said he suffered from a broken heart. The realists assumed Tweedle was a drunk, but in any case, he was believed to have inherited a fortune and he was widely regarded with affection. Tweedle never got in the way, he was always pleasant and polite, and if you got him on the subject of gardening, it turned out he knew more than most.

Shrubs of New England lay open on Tweedle's stomach and responding to Puff's hello, he closed his book and sat upright.

"An interesting fact about holly," he said.

"Holly?" said Puff.

"The holly tree. They sing about it at Christmas. Sharp prickly leaves. The interesting thing about holly is that the leaves are only prickly when the tree is young. It's a self-protection mechanism, you see. As the tree gets older and more established, the leaves round out and soften up so that an elderly holly tree isn't prickly at all. Do you know any women named Holly?"

"Not that I can think of," said Puff.

"Pity. There's a nice story in there somewhere. The sort of thing you could use for a toast on a girl's fiftieth birthday. Provided, of course, that you know a girl named Holly. Enjoy your exercise."

Puff got undressed.

The top three floors of The Avenue Club were devoted to its athletic facilities. There was a small weight room with rowing machines and treadmills, but the lion's share of the space was given over to squash, court tennis and racquets. Court tennis and racquets are such unusual games that even at the Avenue few men know the rules, and Puff had never played either of them. Instead he was a swimmer, and having stripped naked—no one wore trunks—Puff headed down to the beautiful white tiled pool room and hung his towel over the back of a chair.

On a small dais at the far end of the room Dick Burkus lay face down on a table getting a massage.

"Dick," said Puff.

"Puff," Dick grunted.

Dick was a large man with a fat face and a big belly. He had a hairy chest and a hairy back and though he was mostly bald on top, he had large tufts of bright red curly hair around his temples. Dick was the head of the admissions committee at the Avenue Club, and he had known Puff since he was a boy. They had gone to the same boarding school together, they had graduated in the same class at Harvard, and forty years later they were still travelling in the same circles and going to the same cocktail parties. But they had never much liked each other much. Puff thought Dick was vulgar; Dick thought Puff was a bore.

"Jos Nicols," said Puff approaching the dais.

"I'm aware of it."

Jos Nicols was the young member (meaning under 35) who sat on Dick's admissions committee. Jos had been sent to Tokyo for three months just as the club elections were approaching and Puff was concerned about finding a replacement.

Dick groaned as the masseur kneaded his hands into Dick's buttocks.

"I thought Ben Davis would make a good substitute," said Puff. "He's a clever young man. Banker at Lazard, seems to know lots of people. I spoke to him last night and he said he'd be happy to fill in. As you know, we need to have at least one young member on the committee. It's the young members who'll have to live with our decisions and they deserve a voice in the election."

Dick was laid out on the massage table in a way that had him staring directly at Puff's penis. He turned his head away.

"It's my committee Puff. Tell Ben Davis he's off the hook. I've already decided on a replacement. I told Bullard to ask Dante at the office this afternoon."

"Dante?"

"He's your nephew," said Dick. "I thought you'd be pleased."

"Dante's a nice boy but he's not someone I'd put on the admissions committee."

"It's not rocket science for chrissakes, all he has to do is show up. That's right. Oooohh. A little more on the shoulder. God, I'm turning into an old man." Dick turned his head again to stare at Puff's penis once more. "Swim your laps, Puff. Don't worry about what doesn't concern you."

Puff lowered himself into the water, and a moment later Dick got up from the massage table and went back to the dressing room. Both men were annoyed. Of course it didn't make the slightest difference who filled in on the admissions committee, but Puff and Dick were so fed up with each other these days that they could hardly ever meet without some sort of disagreement. It had been like this for almost two years now, and the ill will between them had grown so great that it even had its own monument. This monument was known as the spite pole, and the history behind it requires some explanation.

Besides being members of the same club and sharing many of the same friends, Puff and Dick also owned neighboring estates on the North Shore of Long Island. Dick had eight bedrooms on ten acres, Puff had nine bedrooms on fifteen, and although they had never giggled or shared secrets, each had long made an effort not to antagonize the other, and for decades they managed to bump along amicably and the peace was kept. But then Dick met a freelance journalist named Rebecca Holland and fell in love.

For Dick this presented a problem. He didn't want to marry Rebecca because there was always the possibility of divorce, and having been divorced twice, he knew how expensive it was. But at the same time Dick loved Rebecca and he very much wanted her to live with him as if she were his wife. He had convinced her to move into his apartment in the city, but he couldn't persuade her to spend the summer months at his house on Long Island. Rebecca didn't mind visiting for the occasional weekend but she refused to stay longer than that, and with good reason.

In the first place Rebecca was a woman with a life of her own and she didn't wish to give up her independence if Dick was unwilling to marry her. In the second place, Rebecca knew enough about life at Dick's summer house to conclude that it was very often a pain in the ass.

The upkeep of Dick's estate called for three full time servants — a maid, a cook and a groundskeeper — and Dick was constantly hiring, firing, and bickering with them. Rebecca hated it, and she suspected, rightly, that if she were to become the woman of the house, the nasty business of managing the staff would get passed on to her. Rebecca wanted no part of that, so she told Dick that she'd only be willing to spend the summers on Long Island if he gave her a place of her own to escape to. "Fine," said Dick. "I'll build you one." There was a large, tumble-down garage a hundred yards from the main house and Dick proposed to have it renovated for her. Which is when the trouble started with Puff.

Puff had nothing particular against Rebecca, but he disapproved of Dick's love life in general, and he was violently opposed to the garage renovation because according to the local zoning, old garages could only be made into new garages. Turning an old garage into a lover's retreat complete with kitchen and two baths was a flagrant violation of the law, and as soon as Puff discovered the plan, he brought a complaint before the town council, forcing the councilmen to vote against the issuance of any construction permits.

Naturally, Dick was furious and his anger only subsided when he hit on the idea of planting of an eighty foot flag pole near the water on the edge of Puff's boundary line. It was within spitting distance of Puff's dock; it flew a giant American flag that waved night and day; and it was so perfectly placed as to stand directly in line of sight between Puff's favorite terrace chair and a picturesque nineteenth century lighthouse across the Long Island Sound.

This was the famous spite pole, and when Puff complained about the obstruction to his view, Dick told him to take his complaint to the town council: "It's the American flag, Puff. See if they don't tell you to stick it up your ass."

Puff swam fifty laps. He pulled himself out of the pool and toweled off. He hoped that Dick was not still in the dressing room.

2

Dante Penfield scratched his head and stared hard at his computer screen. His telephone rang but he didn't answer it. Dante hadn't answered his office phone for going on six months and anyway, he was busy.

Dante was at work on the final scene of his screenplay. He was an avid reader of murder mysteries and his screenplay was a murder mystery, too. It was called *The Darkness of Daisy's Back Passage* and it was the story of a beautiful young woman who marries a rich, old financier and goes to live on his an enormous estate in the Hamptons. Daisy is charming and intelligent but she is also ambitious and cold hearted. Aldous Camp, her husband, is a tightfisted misanthrope who suffers from a heart ailment.

One night Aldous is found dead in the dark passageway leading to the maids' quarters at the back of the house. Is it foul play or simply a heart attack? Daisy stands to inherit a fortune so she immediately falls under suspicion, but if she's guilty of murder she's planned it well. The police can't find anything against her and the detectives are stymied. There's a tense interrogation scene at the end of the first act but Daisy plays it cool. It looks like she'll get off scott free.

After the set-up, the screenplay skips ahead in time. It's a year later and Daisy has transformed herself into a fashionable society hostess. The action picks up during a weekend house party at her newly redecorated estate. Among the many guests is a handsome young man named Caleb Astor whom Daisy hopes to bed. Caleb is a brilliant lawyer but, unbeknownst to all, he's also an amateur sleuth, and out of curiosity he starts investigating the death of Daisy's husband. And although the evidence is merely circumstantial, Caleb comes to the inevitable conclusion that Daisy is a murderess.

Dante pulled his chin. He liked the story so far, but he'd been trying to figure out how it ends for ages and nothing had yet presented itself. The difficulty Dante faced was this: he'd put so much effort into making Daisy commit the perfect crime that when Caleb the amateur sleuth shows up there's no smoking gun left to find. The only way Caleb can establish Daisy's guilt is to trick her into a confession, but how do you trick a beautiful, intelligent woman into confessing murder?

Dante's phone rang again but this time he didn't even hear it. Inspiration was upon him and he was typing as fast as he could.

On Saturday night all the houseguests eat a big dinner and retire to the living room for coffee. Everyone is slightly drunk and the company is casting about for something to do when Caleb blandly suggests they play a game of *I Never*. He explains the rules: it's like *Truth Or Dare* but without the dares. The first player makes an announcement about something they've never done — dyed their hair, stolen candy from a shop, had sex in an airplane—then you go around the room and everyone else has to announce whether or not they've ever done it as well:

```
The guests have played a number of rounds
and the room is filled with laughter. It's
CALEB's turn to start the game.

                    CALEB
      I never killed my husband.

There is an audible gasp as Daisy's guests
look anxiously around at one another.

                    GUEST 1
      I never killed my husband.

                    GUEST 2
      I never killed my husband.

                    GUEST 3
      I never killed my husband.

The tension mounts as it gets closer
and closer to Daisy's turn. Close up on
Daisy. Sweat is pouring down her face.
The room goes deathly quiet.

                    DAISY
      I never killed my... I never killed
      my... All right, yes, I did it! I
      killed my husband!

Two policemen, who've been listening in
from outside the living room, burst in.
Daisy is handcuffed and arrested. Slow
pan out across the Atlantic Ocean. The
desperate loneliness of the water.

                  THE END!!!
```

Dante was so excited to have found an ending for his screenplay that he threw his fists in the air and let out a short yelp. But then he read over what he had just written and realized that it didn't quite work. It didn't work to have Caleb say he never killed his husband because Caleb was a man and he couldn't have a husband. The line would have to be changed. Dante replaced "husband" with "spouse," but it wasn't a perfect solution. Daisy's big confession (*"All right, yes, I did it! I killed my spouse!"*) no longer carried the same punch. Would "partner" be better? Dante wasn't sure what to do, and decided to ask Audrey to read it over when he got home.

The thought of Audrey made Dante sad. She was his roommate and his best friend, and they had lived together for the last three years, but now she was talking about moving to Iowa and Dante found it so depressing that he had vowed not to think about her unless absolutely necessary, and he was briefly angry at himself for the carelessness that allowed her to pop into his head.

"When your phone rings, that means it's for you," said Billy Foster. Billy had the desk next to Dante's and he was leaning over the office partition wall, waving to get Dante's attention.

"I was busy," Dante replied.

Billy laughed. "You never do anything."

"I do, I'm writing a screenplay. You can read it if you want."

Billy shook his head dismissively but there was a queer look of sympathy in his eyes. "Mr. Bullard just called me. He wants to see you."

"But I haven't had my lunch."

"That's up to you. Mr. Bullard said he wants to see you immediately. He's waiting in his office."

Old Money

Mr. Bullard was the founder of *Bullard & Associates*, the commercial real estate firm for which Dante worked, and he was a close friend of Dante's uncle Puff. The friendship was based largely on the fact that Puff was a reliable source of capital, but that didn't make it any less genuine. Mr. Bullard had come to respect Puff's judgement a great deal over the years and he'd been happy to give Dante the job.

Dante walked down the hall to Mr. Bullard's office and knocked on the open door.

"Come in and close the door. Have a seat."

Dante did as asked, and looking around Mr. Bullard's office he was impressed once again by how plainly furnished it was. Just a metal desk and a few creaky filing cabinets. Mr. Bullard was from an old New England family; he didn't believe in ostentation.

"A little club business first," said Mr. Bullard. "Do you know Jos Nichols? He's on the admissions committee and he's just been sent to Japan. That leaves us without a young member for the spring election, and Dick Burkus wants to know if you'd be willing to fill in. Would you mind? It doesn't require much, just two meetings and you'll get a good dinner out of it."

"That's fine," said Dante.

"Good, I'll tell Dick you've agreed. Now there's something else I'd like to talk to you about, but before I begin I was just wondering whether you know what it is. I spoke to your uncle last week, and I thought he might have passed on the gist of our conversation." Here Mr. Bullard picked up a pencil and started rolling back and forth between his thumb and forefinger. "No? Nothing? Fair enough, it's about your career, Dante. I get the sense you're not happy here."

"I'm perfectly happy," said Dante.

"No, not happy at all. That's the feeling I get, and that's what I told Puff when he asked me how you were doing: disengaged and not happy at all. Your uncle was concerned, Dante, and he's a intelligent man. He's given me a lot of good advice over the years and one thing he's always said to me: every man ends up spending most of his life at the office, and it's only bearable if what he does at the office is something he truly loves."

Well, that certainly sounded like something Uncle Puff would say. He was a great one for talking about the love of work and the dignity of labor. He often said that if fate ever turned against him and he became a street sweeper, he'd be the best damn street sweeper you'd ever seen. It was one of those hypotheticals that Dante sometimes yearned to see tested out in real life.

"Look the question I'm getting at, Dante, is this: do you love commercial real estate? I don't think you do."

"Does anyone love commercial real estate?" asked Dante. "Do you?"

Mr. Bullard answered carefully. "I like it a lot. I care deeply about it." Then he folded his arms across his chest as if daring to be disbelieved, and for half a minute Dante was genuinely puzzled. He hadn't anticipated this discussion and he stared at Mr. Bullard trying to imagine what it meant to care deeply about commercial real estate. There was an embarrassing silence before Dante realized what was going on.

"I'm being stupid, aren't I?"

"A bit," said Mr. Bullard.

"Yes, I suppose so. I'm sorry Mr. Bullard."

"Please don't take it badly, there's nothing to apologize for.

It's just a matter of being fair. You haven't even lifted a finger since you got here and it doesn't sit well with the other employees. I hope you understand my position."

"Completely."

"That's very good of you." Mr. Bullard brightened. "You know, I have a lot of affection for you, Dante. And of course I have the greatest admiration for your Uncle Puff. I wouldn't like him to think I was pushing you out the door against your wishes."

"Not to worry. I'll clear out my desk today, and I'll tell Puff I quit."

"No hard feelings?"

"None at all."

Mr. Bullard visibly relaxed. He stopped fiddling with his pencil and stood up to shake Dante's hand. He actually tried to hug him. "Just out of curiosity," he said, "What have you been doing all this time?"

"Writing a screenplay," Dante replied. "Just finished in fact. Want to read it?"

"No thank you," said Mr. Bullard quickly. "But it's been a pleasure, and I suppose I'll see you at Trixie's Garden Party tomorrow."

"Until tomorrow," said Dante.

"And give my best to Puff."

"Best to Puff."

Dante closed the office door behind him and Mr. Bullard breathed a sigh of relief. Dante was a decent young man and Mr. Bullard resolved to do him a favor if the opportunity ever arose, even if it was nothing more than signing a few drinks to his chit at the club.

3

Audrey Camp (it was her surname that Dante had given to the corpse in his movie) was sprawled out on the love seat in the living room, her head propped against one armrest and her feet not quite reaching the other. She took a sip of coffee and turned another page of her novel. Audrey was a small girl with light brown hair, pretty green eyes and a pleasant openness to her face that was in contrast with the harder line suggested by the black on black outfits she habitually wore. Audrey was a graduate student in English at Columbia University. She taught two sections of a survey course on 19th century literature while at the same time she was finishing up a master's thesis on the poet Philip Larkin: *They fuck you up, your mum and dad./ They may not mean to, but they do.* Audrey could admire the verse without sharing the sentiment. She was from Ohio and had always liked her parents.

"Pink or lime green?" asked Dante, stepping into the living room and holding out two ties for inspection. Audrey grimaced. "It's a formal lunch," Dante protested, "I have to wear a tie."

"You can't have to wear one of those. Look at yourself, Dante. I don't know why you think you have to dress like a popsicle to create an effect."

"First of all," said Dante enjoying himself, "I don't dress like a popsicle, and second of all, there's nothing I can do about it. You may laugh at yellow linen trousers, but you'd laugh a lot harder if you saw me in dungarees and a black leather jacket."

"People don't say *dungarees* anymore."

"My uncle Puff does. Anyway, you know what I mean."

"Wear the pink, then."

Dante went to the mirror to tie his tie and Audrey's eyes followed him across the room. He was quite right about his clothes. Dante would look even more foolish if he dressed more normally, he'd look phony. Audrey tried hard to picture him in a plaid lumberjack shirt but it couldn't be done, and once again she marveled at the oddity of Dante's world, and the even greater oddity of her having become part of it.

When Audrey moved to New York she never imagined living with a boy who wore yellow linen trousers in an apartment on 89th and Fifth, but that's where she ended up and it was all due to a chance encounter with Dante's mother, whom Audrey met while on holiday three summers ago.

Dante's mother was named Violet, his father (Puff's brother) was dead, and Violet now lived in South Kensington with a retired French chef named Gascon. Violet was English. She'd never felt comfortable in America and she returned home shortly after her husband died, as soon as Dante was old enough to be sent to boarding school. She made up for her absence by writing long letters and sending a case of sherry each year on Dante's birthday, but despite these efforts she still suffered from occasional fits of parental remorse and longing. Left idle for too long, Violet would eventually get round to worrying that she was a bad mother and if the attack was severe enough she might even fly over for a visit. Dante did his best to discourage these episodes, but he had no power to eliminate them entirely, and it was in the middle of one such mother worry attack that Violet discovered Audrey. They met on an Edinburgh-to-London train, and Audrey was so calmly reassuring that when she subsequently let slip that she was starting at Columbia in the fall, Violet immediately suggested she take one of the spare bedrooms on 89th Street. As Violet said:

"Dante needs someone to look after him."

Audrey's duties were never officially spelled out, but the informal understanding was that she would keep the apartment in decent order (not much of a chore since Lativia came twice a week), make sure the bills got paid (with Violet's money), and in return she could live rent free in a large four bedroom next to the park.

The deal worked out nicely for everyone. Audrey liked the apartment, and Dante liked having her around. Dante liked her for so many different reasons that he had trouble listing them all. For one thing Audrey was a girl, and never having known many girls it made Dante feel more properly grown up to live with one. For another, she was a fantastic girl and probably his best friend in the world. And then on top of everything else, Audrey had a particularly good effect on Dante's relations with his mother. She hadn't been to visit in ages.

"Have you read this?" asked Audrey, holding up her novel.

"*Paisley Mischief*," Dante grinned. "Hot tamale, isn't it?"

Old Money

"It's a real skewering of your uncle Puff's Long Island set. I'm surprised they're not up in arms."

"Oh, they are. Give it to me for a second. Listen to this."

Audrey handed Dante the book and he turned to page eighty-six, which he had dog-eared in his head. Dante read out loud:

Charlie Taylor was a fat, balding man with a bulbous nose, sagging cheeks and red curly hair around his temples. He was the quintessential product of an Ivy League education and his brain was equally divided between bore and lech. The boring half of Charlie's brain was used as storage for opinions printed on the editorial page of the *Wall Street Journal*; the lecherous half was used as a sort of appointment book, filled up with a long list of names and dates in which Charlie kept track of the where, when and how of every woman he had ever propositioned. He put a mental asterisk next to his successes and a little black mark next to the failures.

The biggest black mark of all was next to Sarah Davis' name. She was the wife of Charlie's college roommate and he was visiting their house in Maine one weekend when Sarah decided to teach him the art of picking wild mushrooms. After a long walk through the woods, she found a patch of edible mushrooms and knelt down to pick them. While she was staring at the ground, Charlie quickly dropped his trousers around his ankles and when she next looked up, Sarah found herself staring at a stiff red pecker that was poking out from underneath Charlie's enormous belly. She screamed and pushed him away, causing Charlie to lose his balance and fall heavily into a patch of poison ivy.

"His testicles," Sarah Davis reported to her friends, "Swelled up to the size of beach balls."

"Remember Dick Burkus, the spite pole man I told you about? It's him to a tee," said Dante. "Mother told me that story when I was a teenager. She was laughing so hard she almost peed her pants."

"Less funny if you're him though," Audrey replied. "I bet he's livid about the book."

"Oddly enough, not. Dick was the first one to recommend I buy a copy. He seems to think it's very funny."

"Perhaps he likes seeing himself as a young goat. Is he still like that?"

"I don't really know, but I assume he's slowed down. He's got that younger journalist woman now, Rebecca, the one he wanted to remodel the garage for."

"Ughh," said Audrey. "I wonder what the attraction is on her side. Is it just money?"

"Possibly money, but it's hard to say. Mystery of love I suppose."

"Has Puff read *Paisley Mischief*?"

"God, no. Puff is outraged. He caught me with it at the club last week and gave me a scolding. He says it's all malicious gossip, refuses to even look at it. He says whoever wrote it is a real *blankety blank*."

"A *blankety blank*?"

"Exactly that." It was an iron rule with Puff that he never used foul language.

Audrey shook her head. "So who wrote it? One of Puff's friends?"

"Well that's just it, no one knows. The jacket says Anne

Smith, but that's a pen name. The real author's anonymous and everyone's trying to figure out who it is."

"Don't you have any ideas?" asked Audrey.

Dante took a sip of her coffee before answering. "There are two rumors I've heard. One possibility is someone named Andrew Draper. He rents a cottage from Dolly Smith in Oyster Bay and since Dolly's a notorious gossip and Draper's her tenant, the thinking is that he could have picked up the stories from her. Also, the pen name sort of works out. Andrew Draper plus Dolly Smith, Anne Smith."

"Too convenient. Draper's probably a retired accountant."

"A retired insurance salesman actually. Now he collects antiques."

"And I bet he never thought of writing a book in his life. Why not Dolly Smith herself? If she knows all the gossip maybe she's wrote it."

"Unlikely. Dolly's a talker not a novelist. She's an old friend of mother's and as mother would say, she's a goose. I don't think Dolly's read a book since she left high school. Hard to see how she could write one."

"So who else is there?"

"The other rumor is much more intriguing," said Dante. "I got it from Trixie, Puff's wife. She's read *Paisley Mischief* cover to cover three times over and her guess is Dick's girlfriend wrote it. Makes sense in a way. A lot of the dirt could have come directly from Dick, and Rebecca's been around long enough to collect plenty herself. She's a journalist so it's no stretch to imagine her writing a novel. The only difficulty is figuring out why she'd write such a nasty portrait of Dick."

"Perhaps she thinks it's funny, like he does," said Audrey. "Or maybe his randiness turns her on."

"Are women really like that?"

"Not mostly. Occasionally they are."

Dante drank the last of Audrey's coffee.

"I've got to get going. The fund raiser starts at twelve thirty. Are you going to be home when I get back?"

"No," said Audrey. "Didn't you hear Cecil's message on the machine? He's in town. I'm meeting him at the museum then we're going out to dinner."

"What time?"

"We're meeting at three."

"Oh," said Dante, failing to hide his disappointment. "Say hello to him for me."

Cecil Biddle was a mutual friend. Cecil's mother was an acquaintance of Violet's and Dante had known him all his life. Audrey had only known him since meeting Dante, but it was typical of Cecil that he would focus on the girl. Cecil worked in the movie business. He was tall and handsome, with jet black hair, clear blue eyes and a missing pinkie finger on his left hand. Even sensible types tended to swoon, and the missing pinkie was icing on the cake. It made Cecil appear both tough and vulnerable at the same time.

Dante left the living room to collect his wallet, keys and watch. He brushed his hair for a final time and gave the knot of his tie a last tug. He was halfway out of the apartment before he remembered about *The Darkness of Daisy's Back Passage* and he turned back to ask Audrey a final question.

"Did you get a chance to read the ending of my screenplay?"

"Yes."

"What did you think?" Dante waited. "You didn't like it?"

"I didn't say that."

"But you didn't, did you? Why not?"

"Well, think for a minute. Here's Daisy, this clever, sophisticated woman who's gone to the trouble of concocting the perfect way to kill her husband, then all of a sudden she starts playing a game of *I Never* and she blurts out the confession that's going to ruin her life: *'Yes, I killed my spouse!!'*"

"You don't like the word spouse?"

"It's more than that."

"You don't like the whole idea of the parlor game?"

"I don't."

"Damn," said Dante. "Me neither, it's just not believable. I was hoping you wouldn't notice."

"Sorry."

"Not to worry. There are lots of pebbles on the beach. I'll just have to think up something better."

"There you go," said Audrey.

"Have fun with Cecil."

Dante was down the elevator and out on the street by the time the telephone rang. It was Violet calling from London. She told Audrey she had some business to attend to in New York and would be flying over within the next few days. Then the line went silent for a moment and Violet took a deep breath:

"I'm concerned about Dante."

"What about him?"

"Do you think he misses me terribly?"

4

The air was crisp, the sky was clear and a warm sun shone down on the large white tent that had been set up on the front lawn of the Penfields' Long Island home. The weather had cooperated. It was the perfect day for Trixie Penfield's garden party and Trixie herself was hard at work underneath the large white party tent, directing a group of Ecuadorian laborers on the placement of tables, chairs, podiums, and the vast number of plants she had ordered in for the occasion.

"Esto alla y esto alla and esto right by the table over there. Moo buena, gracias."

Trixie liked saying "gracias." It gave her a thrill to converse with the workers in their own language, and of course they were too polite to point out that the job would go much quicker if she just spoke English. It never occurred to Trixie that the nice brown men could speak English.

"Mommy!" said Cat, kissing her mother on the cheek.

"Cómo estás, darling?"

Cat looked around the tent and goggled: "This is crazy!"

Old Money

Cat Penfield was one of those few people who can say "This is crazy!" and really mean it. She was much younger than you'd expect for an only child whose mother who was in her fifties and whose father was well past sixty. Cat was only twenty-two, and although she'd been studying as a serious actress for some time, she still had an innocent quality that seemed a perfect match to her girlish beauty. She had strawberry blonde hair, big blue eyes and a truly marvelous figure.

"Is that what you're wearing?" asked Trixie. Trixie herself was in her work clothes, black linen trousers and a striped French sailor shirt, but she intended to dress for the party. Cat was wearing a simple blue frock, but she had only come out for the day and it wasn't clear whether she'd brought something else to change into.

"Don't you like it? It's all I've got," said Cat.

"I was hoping you'd dress up, but it doesn't matter. No, it's perfect, dear. You look gorgeous. Very natural and casual. You'll disarm him."

"Who's him?" asked Cat.

But Trixie was still thinking over the blue frock. "You'll have to put on some lipstick. It's no use looking too natural. You can take one of the reds from my dressing table upstairs."

"Who's him? A boy?" Cat was shy and she didn't like her mother arranging her dates. It wasn't feminist.

"Not a boy," said Trixie, "That's your business. I'm talking about Max, Max Guberstein. He's a close friend of ours. He's an important movie producer and he could be very helpful to your career. I want you to make a good impression."

Cat bit her lip. "But I hate that kind of stuff, Mom. I never know what to say."

"Nonsense," Trixie replied firmly. "All you've got to do is smile and be yourself. It's just what I've always told you, Cat, men admire women who know how to listen. Max will do the talking and I'm quite certain he's going to like you. He's been wanting to meet you for ages, so don't worry. Go on upstairs and find some lipstick while I finish the arrangements."

With just an hour to go before the guests arrived, the tent had become a whirlwind of activity. In addition to the crew of laborers, there was now a large team of caterers rushing about, setting the tables for lunch. One of the caterers was a tall young man with a bleached blonde crew cut and earrings in both ears. His name was Greg, and he and another boy were laying down silverware just a few feet to Trixie's left. Greg told a joke which Trixie overheard.

"How do you fake an orgasm with your boyfriend? Spit on his back!"

Trixie refused to laugh, but she allowed herself a little inward giggle and patted herself on the back for being so with it. Some hostesses would have scolded the young man but not Trixie; she was more worldly than people knew.

She clapped her hands and called over three of the Ecuadorians. "Ahora el bamboo en el pole," she said pointing to a huge pile of bamboo shoots in the corner of the tent. Miming furiously, Trixie went on to explain that she wanted the bamboo shoots wrapped around all the metal tent poles to cover them up. It was something she'd once seen done at a wedding in Hobe Sound. It would add a touch of warmth and help create the dense jungle atmosphere that Trixie was aiming for.

The reason for the jungle theme was because the luncheon was in support of the Balawala Elephant Sanctuary Park in Tanzania, of which Trixie was on the board. Before meeting Puff, Trixie was an estate tax lawyer—they fell in love while working out the details of a nifty tax avoidance trust for Puff's dying mother—but since getting married she spent the bulk of her time doing charitable work, and the Balawala Sanctuary was the cause closest to her heart. It was 49,000 acres of pristine wilderness, crowded with all manner of wildlife, and whenever she thought of the elephants wandering through the parkland in ever dwindling numbers, she was moved almost to tears. It was tragic to know that the fate of such noble creatures rested yet on a knife edge, and it was in order to symbolize the precariousness of their plight that she had chosen as the centerpiece for each table a small, porcelain elephant figurine, the bud of a white rose delicately balanced on its tusks.

At last the tent was ready and Trixie surveyed it approvingly. Everything was just as she'd hoped. It would be like lunching in the clearing of a tropical forest. More or less. People don't eat lobster bisque and rack of lamb in the clearings of tropical forests, but Trixie was a realist and she knew that she couldn't ask her friends for $1,000 a plate and serve them chicken salad. Trixie went upstairs to change, and as she walked away, Greg, the blonde caterer, studied the décor and made his own assessment:

"The guests will need a fucking machete to get to the buffet."

It was just past noon when Dante turned left at the entrance to Puff's property and drove slowly up the long pebble drive-way towards the main house.

"Hello?" There was no answer at the front door. "Hello?"

Cat was putting on lipstick, Trixie was upstairs getting dressed and Puff still wasn't back from the golf course. Dante wandered out to the terrace where the caterers had set up a bar.

"Is it too early for a drink?"

"What would you like?" replied the bartender.

"Scotch on the rocks with a splash of water."

Dante sipped his drink. He remained standing at the bar because there was nowhere else to go.

"Do you know what's for lunch?"

"Lobster bisque, rack of lamb and wild berry tart."

"Lovely."

This exhausted Dante's supply of conversation so he looked first at his watch and then off into the distance. He raised an eyebrow and puckered his lips slightly, as if to say, *Hmmm*. This was an habitual pose of his which he often adopted when he felt a touch of social awkwardness. The idea was to convey the impression that he was distracted by some philosophical consideration of great import.

Dante was relieved of his pose by the arrival of a second guest. The new guest was a short, coarse looking man whom Dante didn't recognize. He had a large nose, acne scarred cheeks and he was dressed in a patterned, knit shirt of the sort one rarely saw on Puff's terrace. The man looked angry. He was pounding his fist into his palm and from a distance he appeared to be yelling at himself through clenched teeth. As he came closer Dante saw that he was actually talking into a cell phone attached to his ear.

"Tell him to go to hell!" the man shouted, ripping the phone off his ear and stuffing it into his pocket.

"Hi," said Dante. "I'm Dante Penfield."

"Max Guberstein. I guess I'm early."

"That's alright. Have a drink."

"Club soda with lime," said Max.

"Don't you want a proper drink?"

"I don't drink alcohol, if that's what you mean. It's a bad habit and it disagrees with my stomach."

"Well then," said Dante, "There you are."

"There *you* are. What did you say your name was again?"

"Dante Penfield."

"Any relation to Wallace?"

"Wallace?"

"Wallace Penfield," said Max curtly. It was like pulling teeth with some people. "The man who owns this house."

"Wallace? Oh, you mean Puff. Yes, of course, I'm his nephew. I call him Puff, that's what confused me. Actually, everyone calls him Puff. He prefers it."

Max frowned. Having met Wallace "Puff" Penfield on three previous occasions, he had heard the nickname before but he didn't like using it. Max could not believe that anyone would willingly embrace such a nickname. To call oneself Puff was ridiculous, even pathetic in a way, like introducing yourself to a stranger and saying: "Hi, I'm David but everyone calls me *Shitforbrains*."

Max was silent for a moment as he looked around in search of a change of subject. His eye caught the flag waving down by the water.

"That's a big flag he's got there."

"Oh, it's not Puff's. That's the spite pole."

"The spite pole?"

"Dick Burkus put it up," said Dante. "He owns the next house over. He had a fight with Puff a few years ago and he installed the flag pole just to annoy him, to block his view. Personally, I don't mind it. I think it looks nice.

"You spend a lot of time out here?"

"Not anymore," Dante replied. "I used to when I was a boy. My mother owns the neighboring cottage but I haven't been there in ages. It's all closed up. Mother used to rent it out but now Uncle Puff pays her to keep it empty. He says he doesn't want a group of strangers living so close by."

Dante pointed to a spot of trees a few hundred yards away.

"You can't see the cottage from here but it's just down the hill. We spent the summers there before my father died. I used to have my own a vegetable garden in the back and then I built a tree house in the elm tree outside my bedroom. It had a trap door to get in and out."

Max had been interested in the spite pole but Dante's mention of the tree house killed his patience. He walked away grumbling that he had phone calls to make. The bartender looked at Dante sympathetically: "I used to have a tree house, too."

Soon Trixie's guests started arriving in numbers and the terrace filled up. Puff was back from the golf course and he'd changed into a seersucker suit for the occasion. He tracked Dante down near the bird fountain.

"Hello Puff," said Dante.

Old Money

Puff sighed and shook his head back and forth; he cleared his throat; he grimaced. To Dante, the dumbshow suggested that he was in for a lecture about his failure in the commercial real estate business, and he was right. Puff was very disappointed. Puff had reached the stage in life where one of the few pleasures left to him was that of helping younger men like Dante get along, and it annoyed him to no end when his efforts weren't fully appreciated. If your uncle gets you a job, you're obligated to keep it, and Puff was slowly working up to a speech that would almost certainly include a line about the moral duty which accompanies privilege, when his train of thought was suddenly interrupted by the appearance of a Professor Hurston, the newest member of the Balawala board and an expert zoologist who was scheduled to deliver the afternoon's keynote speech.

"Mr. Penfield? I wanted to introduce myself, I'm Geoff Hurston."

"It's nice to meet you," said Puff, effortlessly switching gears, "Hurston, you say? Geoff Hurston? Let me think."

As soon as Puff put his finger to his lips, Dante knew he was off the hook. The finger on the lips was a sign. It was the opening salvo in Puff's favorite conversational game, something Dante called *Small World*. The object of the game was discover that the stranger you were meeting for the first time was in fact related to somebody you already knew.

"Where did you go to school?" asked Puff. "I used to know a Stapley Hurston at Radcliffe. I believe she married an Argentine."

"I'm afraid I don't know her," said the Professor lightheartedly.

"There was a George Hurston at St. Paul's. His family was from Connecticut."

"My family's from Kansas."

"The Kansas Hurstons? Are you sure?"

"By way of Minnesota, they were homesteaders."

"That's no good at all," mumbled Puff. His game was ruined and he looked at the Professor somewhat warily. "Well, it's wonderful what you're doing for the elephants. I must get myself a drink."

Across the terrace, Trixie stood in the middle of a group of five women discussing the book that was on everyone's mind, *Paisley Mischief*. All the women in Trixie's group were well past fifty, but they were all still slender and they were all dressed in clothes that could have been worn by girls half their age. Hemlines were above the knee (because even after the tummy goes you've still got your legs) and blouses were cut low enough to show off the hint of cleavage created by a good support bra. The group was composed of three straw blondes, Trixie among them, one brunette and an elegant grey haired woman named Lala Furstenberg. From a distance the women might have attracted the sexual interest of a college boy and it was only when you got up close that the ravages of time were fully revealed: the swollen knuckles, the loose flaps of skin under the arms, and the telltale scars of the surgeon's knife around the chin. One of the women, Nana Johnson, had recently recovered from her third face lift and although Trixie said she looked much better for it, she was being kind. Nana's face looked like pizza dough stretched across a bongo drum.

"I think the book is a disgrace," said Nana.

"You've read it?" asked Trixie.

"Only in parts."

Nana had read the book from cover to cover, but she didn't wish to discuss its contents in detail. There was a story in chapter six about an older woman trying to seduce her daughter's boyfriend and it was uncomfortably similar to a nasty rumor that had once gone round about Nana herself.

"I don't know what the fuss is about," said Lala. "I liked the book. It's just good fun. A little farfetched at times but that's the novelist's prerogative."

Lala was a straight arrow. She wasn't party to the gossip upon which the book was based, so she was able to enjoy it without misgiving. It never occurred to her that the characters might be drawn from her friends.

"I wish we knew who wrote it," said Pookie Wright. "The story I heard, it's the man who rents from Dolly Smith."

"I heard that, too," said Trixie.

"What about Rebecca Holland?" said Nana. "Dick Burkus' girlfriend. Trixie told me she could've written it."

"Well she could have," said Trixie. "After all, she's a journalist so she must know how to write, but I was guessing. There's no inside information. I don't know who wrote the book, and I doubt anyone else does either. It doesn't really matter anyway. We're talking about a novel, not a police report."

"Huh," said Pookie. She couldn't believe that Trixie felt as blasé as she was pretending to. Pookie had studied *Paisley Mischief* fairly closely and she strongly suspected that the central couple was based on Trixie and Puff. Trixie came off all right, but Puff was painted as a monstrous buffoon, and it didn't make sense to Pookie that a woman would react so philosophically in the face of her husband's public humiliation.

"Look," said Nana, pointing a finger in the direction of the bar.

All the women turned their heads at once and saw Rebecca Holland standing with a glass of white wine in her hand, talking to Petra Zaff.

"Do you know what I heard?" said Petra in a whisper, "Trixie thinks you wrote *Paisley Mischief*." Rebecca looked surprised. "Well, did you?"

"No, I didn't."

And at that moment Rebecca looked across the terrace and caught Trixie's eye. Trixie waved to her and Rebecca wandered over.

"We were just talking about you," said Trixie. "I love your outfit."

"Thanks," said Rebecca.

Trixie kissed her warmly on both cheeks while Nana Johnson watched with a cynical eye. Like everyone else, Nana knew that Puff and Dick were feuding, and she assumed that Trixie and Rebecca disliked each other as much as their men did. But Nana was small minded. There was no hint of sham in Trixie's affectionate greeting. Trixie was her own woman, and she refused to let Puff's peevishness influence her relationship with Rebecca. Trixie had a very sensible attitude towards other peoples' feuds: she ignored them. Her world was too small for taking sides. Everyone Trixie knew had disagreements with someone about something, and if she allowed herself to fight with all the people her friends were fighting with, she would be left with no one to talk to.

"It's a pity Dick couldn't be here," said Trixie. "But it was good of him to send you, and please give him my thanks for the contribution, won't you?"

"He was happy to do it."

Rebecca was shading the truth. Dick's sentiment was better summed up by the phrase he used when Rebecca first told him she wanted to attend Trixie's party.

"Goddamn bullshit."

Dick distrusted philanthropy and it pained him to give $1,000 to an elephant park in Africa. Every year he donated to the endowment of his boarding school, but he didn't like giving money to anyone else. Dick believed that trying to solve other people's problems was a waste of time and he felt the same way about elephants. They'd always be bitching about something.

But Dick wrote the check anyway because Rebecca insisted, and because he knew that her desire to go had nothing to do with African wildlife. Rebecca had two objects in mind. First, she wanted to pick up the latest chatter for a piece she was working on about *Paisley Mischief*. And second, she wanted to meet Max Guberstein. Rebecca had written for the glossy magazines for years, but each new article meant a lot of effort and you never got much credit for it. Rebecca wanted a change, Max could provide one, and she had good reason to believe he would go out of his way to be helpful.

"Where's Mr. Guberstein?" she said to Trixie. "Can you point him out to me?"

"Come along. I'll introduce you."

Max was then sipping his second club soda with Cat Penfield on his left and a woman named Budgie Bowles on his right. Budgie was much taller than Max and she was speaking excitedly down at Max while he scowled up at her. Budgie had just discovered that Max was a movie producer, and she was telling him about a wonderful idea she had for a television travel series. The idea came to her during a visit to Bilbao. Budgie sent a photograph of herself in front of the Guggenheim Museum to her mother in Connecticut and on the back she'd written, "Me, in Spain!"

"Don't you think that's the perfect title for a television series?" said Budgie. "Me, In Spain! It really captures the excitement of travel and if it catches on, you could keep it up forever. Me, In France! Me, In Scotland!"

Me, Up My Own Ass! thought Max, relieved to see Trixie coming to his rescue.

"I hope I'm not interrupting," Trixie said airily. She was a practiced hostess, and in the blink of an eye she had drawn Cat and Budgie away, leaving Max alone with Rebecca. Trixie squeezed Cat's hand gently and waited until they were out of earshot.

"You see?" said Trixie, "I knew Max would like you. What did you talk about?"

"I told him about the play I'm in, *Room 421.*"

"And was he interested?"

"Yes, very," Cat answered happily. "He's going to send one of his scouts to see the show. He says I have potential."

"You've got him wrapped around your finger, darling."

"You really think so?"

"Of course I do."

By the time lunch was announced Rebecca and Max were fast friends. They had exchanged business cards and Max told her to call whenever she felt like it. He also asked her to pass on his best wishes to Dick. "I'm having dinner with him next week. Tell him I'm looking forward to it."

"I certainly will," said Rebecca smiling gratefully.

There was a brief tumult as the guests bounced around in search of their table seatings, and at the end of it Dante found himself at the back of the tent squeezed in next to Mr. Bullard. They ate their rack of lamb in modest silence, and it was not until the main course was being cleared that Mr. Bullard ventured into a discussion of the Avenue Club and Dante's new position on the admissions committee.

"I suppose you met Max Guberstein," said Mr. Bullard. "What did you think of him?"

"I don't know. Rather odd, I guess, at least in context of Puff's terrace. Is he a friend of yours?"

"Well, yes, in a way." Mr. Bullard turned serious, lowering his voice. "But he's much more a friend of your Uncle Puff's. You're on the committee now, so I think you should know that Max is up for election at the club this spring. And Puff wants him to get in."

Mr. Bullard cocked his head meaningfully, but Dante's surprise was so great that the gesture was wasted. Dante felt certain he must have misheard, however there was no chance to ask a follow up because just at that moment Puff stepped up to the podium and tapped the microphone loudly with his finger, signaling the beginning of the speeches.

Puff's job was to introduce Professor Hurston and he kept it admirably short. Professor Hurston, who'd been tasked to give a lecture on species preservation, was equally kind and somehow managed to get through the whole subject in less than ten minutes. But then it was Trixie's turn and the program ground to halt, the heavy flow of her words creating a soporific blanket that spread over the entire tent. Trixie began with a detailed description of her own experiences visiting Balawala, segued into a general discussion of the mythic symbolism of wild animals, and closed with the reading of a long poem she had written for the occasion.

> In darkest Africa where wild things roam,
> The noble elephant is losing his home,
> Day and night he wanders around,
> Searching for protected ground.

That was the first stanza, but there were many more like it, and when the poem finally came to an end, it was unclear whether the applause was for the poet or the poet's silence. Trixie blushed proudly and continued on in a new vein:

"Now for what is perhaps the most important part of our gathering today. I want to thank each and every one of you for your support of the Balawala Elephant Sanctuary. You have all been very generous but I want especially to thank Mr. Max Guberstein whose unexpected gift was more than I could have hoped for." Trixie paused to point Max out to the crowd. "Max is a true lover of wildlife and I feel honored to be his friend. It is thanks to him, and to everyone else who came today, that the elephants of Tanzania can sleep more soundly tonight. Thank you."

There was another long round of applause and the lunch was over, the guests began to disperse.

Dante lingered over the crumbs of his wild berry tart. He wondered how come he knew so many people who wrote after-dinner poetry. Then his curiosity fell on Max Guberstein. It was strange to discover that Max was so close to Puff and Trixie. Why had Dante never heard of him before?

5

The night after his dinner with Audrey, Cecil Biddle woke up in his hotel room at the Soho Grand to the sound of his cell phone ringing. The alarm clock flashed 6:35. He had a dry mouth and a touch of headache. There was a small whirlpool in his stomach.

To Cecil these were not the symptoms of hangover, they were the symptoms of morning, and he tolerated them without complaint because he knew that without a large glass of whiskey before bed he was incapable of falling asleep. Far better to wake up with dry mouth and a funny tummy than to meet the new day without having slept.

"Cat piss," said Cecil.

This was an expression he had adopted fairly recently. He'd picked it up from a news report on television. A white schoolgirl in rural Mississippi had described her home town as "pure cat piss" and Cecil liked the sound of it so much that it was now the first thing out of his mouth every morning. He didn't use the phrase in reference to anything in particular, but rather as a candid appraisal of his life in general. Cecil was in the movie business.

Cecil was in the movie business not because he had an artistic temperament or because he loved movies, he was in it because he thought it was the only thing he was fit for. He didn't have the brains to be a lawyer, or the dedication to be a doctor, but he did possess a natural grace and a knack for making higher-ups like him, which in the movie business was plenty. Cecil still couldn't quite believe it. He'd been working in film for almost four years and he hadn't been found out yet.

Cecil worked for GoldStream Pictures and officially he was a Vice-President, but the job wasn't as impressive as it sounded and the official title didn't mean much. If you were to ask Cecil what exactly he was Vice-President of, he would have answered without hesitation: *Max Guberstein's bum.*

Max was the President of GoldStream Pictures and Cecil was his personal assistant. He was really nothing more than an errand boy, and although he had a large expense account and earned a shocking amount of money, he was paid to be a toady. He carried Max's briefcase, ordered Max's lunch, arranged Max's social life and even, on occasion, tidied up after him in the bathroom.

This last humiliation occurred during a dinner with investors at a private home in Lake Tahoe a few months ago. It was a bitter memory and Cecil preferred not to dwell on it. Max went to the bathroom and when he returned to the dinner table he whispered in Cecil's ear: "I left some nastiness in the toilet bowl. I want you to take care of it."

From Max's point of view, it was a perfectly reasonable request. If Max spent the time to clean the toilet himself, his absence might be remarked upon at dinner ("What's he doing in there?"). On the other hand, if he left the bowl dirty and someone else followed him into the bathroom, he might be accused of bad manners ("That horrid man who left his mess all over the john!"). The logic was irrefutable, and besides, Cecil got paid a great deal of money to deal with such problems.

Cecil was in a double bind. He not only hated his job, he was also worried about losing it, and by his own calculations he had little more than two months of employment left, three months tops. This wasn't because Cecil was a bad errand boy, it was simply in the nature of things. Max disliked people on the whole and he was incapable of tolerating the company of any one person for longer than a year. Max had never kept a personal assistant much past the first anniversary and Cecil was already going ten months.

So Cecil knew he was on the verge of getting fired, and for those who'd served as *Vice-President of Max Guberstein's Bum* there were only two paths open to them. The unlucky ones got fired and Max called everyone he knew to make sure they would never work in the industry again. The lucky ones also got fired, but Max would sometimes help them find another job before saying goodbye. Cecil wanted to be lucky. He was eager to say goodbye, but he needed Max's help with that other job, and the reason he needed another job so badly was probably on the other end of the ringing phone line.

She was named Penelope and she was Cecil's girlfriend.

Old Money

They were engaged to be married and they shared a flat in London. Though to be precise, they didn't quite share it. Penelope lived in the flat, and Cecil paid for it. Cecil himself spent most of his time in California, and he only went to London for short visits when his schedule allowed.

Penelope was a formidable young woman. She had blonde hair, porcelain skin and an eye-popping figure which she kept in shape by means of cigarettes, alcohol and yoga. Apart from being beautiful, Penelope was sharp, witty and forthright, and Cecil admired her a great deal, he loved her even, but the engagement notwithstanding, there were serious drawbacks to actually marrying her.

To begin with, Penelope spent money and lots of it. It was not sand through an hourglass, nor water through a sieve, it was wheat gushing out of a grain elevator. Penelope set fire to enormous piles of cash at every chance she got. She wore expensive clothes, threw large parties and redecorated constantly; and Cecil guessed that her tastes would only get more lavish once he became her husband. Cecil couldn't hope to support her on the small income he got from his father and he was unhappy at the thought of having to earn pots and pots just to keep her in stockings.

The other drawback to marrying Penelope was that, despite her charms, she was impossible to live with. At least Cecil thought so. The two of them got on well enough when they had the Atlantic Ocean as a buffer, but make them share a house for more than a three day weekend and they were at each other's throats. If it makes sense to assign blame in such matters, it could be placed on both sides.

Cecil complained that Penelope was stubborn and bossy. She was socially ambitious and she dragged him to endless parties, making him chase after fancy people in whom he had no interest.

Penelope's complaint was more straightforward. It was Cecil's habit of sleeping with girls he wasn't engaged to. He didn't boast of his conquests, but Penelope guessed at what went on and the thought of it, which pressed upon her whenever Cecil was at home for more than a few days, infuriated her.

Given the state of affairs, Cecil was understandably nervous about marrying Penelope, and the only thing that made him more nervous was the thought of breaking up with her. In Cecil's mind, it was the choice between living with a tiger or being eaten by one. Neither choice appealed and for some time now he had pinned his hopes on the thought that by delaying the decision indefinitely a third, more painless, option might present itself. Which was why Cecil was so keen to line up another Hollywood job after Max fired him, because without one, he'd have to go back to London and sort out his life with Penelope.

The phone kept ringing. Cecil sat up in bed, swung his feet onto the floor and rubbed the sleep out of his eyes.

Actually, he enjoyed talking to Penelope on the phone. She was full of gossip, she told a good story, and when he ran into a problem she usually offered sound advice. What Cecil was less pleased about was Penelope's habit of calling so early in the morning. Of course there was the time difference in London to be considered, but it was also true that the six a.m. calls were Penelope's way of figuring out where Cecil had slept and whether he had slept alone. Cecil didn't want to answer but he had to whenever he decently could, if only so as to run out of excuses when he couldn't.

Fortunately, Cecil was clean of conscience this morning. He'd felt a momentary frisson with Audrey the night before, but nothing like two years ago and nothing had come of it. Cecil put a smile on his face and filled his mind with tenderness. He took a deep breath and picked up his cell phone.

"Good morning, sweetie." There was no response. "Sweetie? Good morning?"

Cecil heard a rough hacking cough and then the sound of someone spitting. There was a slight pause and then a bellowing voice screamed into his ear:

"Meeting! Emergency meeting!"

"Hello, Max."

"Right now!"

"The meeting isn't until nine o'clock," said Cecil.

"Pre-meeting meeting! Extremely important. We need to go over some items. I want you here in fifteen minutes."

"Where are you?"

"The Pierre."

"Forty-five minutes. I just woke up." Cecil had learned to haggle with Max. Otherwise he'd swallow you whole.

"Half an hour."

"Half an hour, then."

Cecil slid out of bed. He showered, shaved and dressed, and while brushing his teeth he studied his face in the mirror. He looked tired, still handsome but less so than formerly. Life's pressures were starting to show, and he cursed Max for waking him up for no good reason.

Cecil didn't know why Max needed to see him, but he assumed he was being dragged out of bed without cause because one of the trials of working for Max was that, as much as he disliked people, Max couldn't stand being alone. In all likelihood there would be nothing to discuss at the pre-meeting meeting and certainly nothing of importance. Odds were that Max was just eating breakfast and since he didn't like to sit by himself, he wanted someone there to watch him eat.

"Cat piss," said Cecil.

He went downstairs to hail a cab.

As Cecil made his way to the Pierre, Max was sitting at a large round table in the back of the hotel dining room drinking a cup of herbal tea. Max owned houses in Los Angeles, Colorado and Connecticut, but his legal residence was a suite at the Pierre on Fifth Avenue and 61st Street. He had never owned an apartment in Manhattan because by the time he was rich enough to buy one, he was too old and proud to subject himself to the scrutiny of a co-op board.

Max was approaching sixty, and as has been mentioned, he was the President of GoldStream Pictures. He produced documentary and feature films for both television and theatrical release and he was, by his own estimation, one of the seven most important independent producers in the country. *Variety* had recently published rankings that put him ninth, but *Variety* got their facts wrong. You can't believe what you read in the press.

Old Money

Unlike many of his competitors, Max had never planned on a career in film. Born in Brooklyn, he was the son of a dry cleaner and when his parents died, both of them in quick succession, Max took over the dry cleaning business. Still in his twenties, he turned a single struggling shop into a profitable chain, but Max soon grew bored of dry cleaning and began to look about for new ways to invest his money. When a young film director approached him looking to finance a documentary about the Brooklyn Dodgers, Max put up $100,000.

According to the queer standards of the entertainment industry, a film is a success whenever the investors don't lose their shirts, and according to those standards, the Dodgers documentary was a success. The film was sold to television, the director walked off with a check for $40,000, and Max eventually got his $100,000 back along with a two percent return.

At first Max was quite pleased with himself. Then he reconsidered. He had risked a lot of money on the deal and made a grand total of $2,000. The director, his partner, had risked no money of his own and earned $40,000. Max realized that as a movie investor he'd been cast in the sucker's role, and from there it was only a short step to the realization that the magic of movies was so powerful that there must be lots of people who were willing to play the sucker's role.

The next time the young director came knocking to raise money, Max offered him a deal. Max would find the investors and he would pay the director a decent fee, but in return, Max would get to keep control of all the film's finances and whatever profits were left over. The director accepted the arrangement, the second film was made and although Max's investors lost money, Max himself pocketed a hefty production fee. The experiment was a success and ever since then Max had moved from one triumph to another. His deals had grown ever larger, his projects ever more numerous, but he always avoided paying for anything out of his own pocket and he never let his eye stray from the bottom line.

Max became well known in Hollywood for driving a hard bargain. He didn't waste money and he didn't waste words. In a business where people tend to lay the butter on with a trowel, Max never gave a dollar's worth of flattery for a dime's worth of favors. He did not pat you on the back, he did not gush about your genius, and he did not laugh at your jokes just to make you feel better. As a result he'd won a reputation as a shrewd deal maker, but he'd also won a reputation as a miserable human being. Both were more or less true.

Max sipped his herbal tea and waited impatiently for the day to begin. He was a restless man and he harbored a certain resentment against anyone who was not awake before sunrise. He didn't understand how anyone could sleep more than eight hours at a stretch. Max himself barely managed half that and once his anxiety woke him up, he was unable to fall back asleep and he would pace his rooms like a caged tiger, waiting for the rest of the world to get out of bed. He especially hated the early morning hours because he couldn't make phone calls and to be deprived of making phone calls was, for Max, a form of existential torture. He even had his own name for the pre-dawn period of phonelessness and he referred to it, somewhat melodramatically, as "the darkness."

It was the time between three and six o'clock when no one in either New York or Los Angeles would pick up.

Cecil stood outside the Pierre Hotel smoking a cigarette. He was ten minutes late but he needed to compose himself before entering the dining room.

"Good morning, Max."

"You smell of cigarettes," Max replied. "You know I hate it. Have a mint."

Cecil took the mint and asked the waiter for a menu but Max waved the waiter away.

"I ordered for you. Mineral water and mixed fruit. Now listen carefully, this is important." Max leaned low over the table so that his chin was almost touching the table cloth. "Did you sleep well?"

"Yes, thank you I did." This kind of misdirection was a favorite ploy of Max's but Cecil knew it too well to be phased.

"How's Penelope? Hasn't called off the engagement yet?"

"Not yet."

Max kept close tabs on his employees and it did no good to tell him to mind his own business. Everything was Max's business.

"Of course she hasn't and I'll tell you why. You make a good living. Money is catnip to the ladies."

"Sometimes it is," Cecil's tone was dry. "Not always."

There was a fair amount of give and take in Cecil's relationship with Max. For the most part Cecil felt free to say what he liked and if he was impertinent, even rude, Max didn't hold it against him. Max himself was pushy and plain spoken, and he admired the same qualities in others. He didn't respect people who let themselves be steamrolled. Max insisted on winning his points but he didn't like to win them too easily.

"Crap," said Max. "Money is catnip to everyone. Do you know what an aphorism is?"

"I do."

"Here's an aphorism for you. The difference between comedy and tragedy is this: Comedy is when bad things happen to rich people. Tragedy is when bad things happen to poor people."

"Why did you get me out of bed?"

Max ignored the question. "Let me tell you a joke."

"I've heard it before." Cecil knew this to be true even before the joke was told; Max had a very limited supply.

"A Muslim, a Jew and an Episcopalian watch a beautiful woman ride by on a horse. The Muslim says, What a fine horse! The Jew says, What a fine woman! The Episcopalian — that's you — says, I wonder what her maiden name is?"

"I'm not Episcopalian. I'm English, so I'm Anglican."

"All the same."

The waiter brought over a bottle of mineral water and a bowl of mixed fruit. Cecil pushed the bowl away. "I'd like a Swiss cheese omelet with bacon and white toast. And coffee. Thank you."

"You're killing yourself," said Max.

"I'll keep that in mind. What is this meeting about?"

"Does the name Jack Friend ring a bell?"

"Head of production at Mirror Films."

"Good for you," said Max. "I spoke to Jack last week, and he told me some interesting news. He's looking for someone to run one of his subsidiaries."

54

"SouthEnd Pictures. I saw it in *Variety*. They make films for television."

"I see you've got your ear to the ground," said Max. "It might suit you. No big budgets but the chance to develop your own projects. A good opportunity. Jack asked me if I could recommend anyone."

"Oh?" said Cecil.

"I thought it was something you might be able to do and I gave him your name. Jack wants a meeting, but I told him he'd have to wait a few weeks. There's a little project I need to wrap up before you start looking at other opportunities."

"What project is that?"

Cecil drank his coffee while Max played with his teacup. They looked at each other like poker players trying to decide who held the better cards. Max said:

"Have you ever heard of the Avenue Club?"

"I have."

"What do you think of it?"

"I don't have an opinion. It's just a club."

"Wrong," said Max, "It's *the* club, the most exclusive in the city."

Cecil raised an eyebrow at that. He had nothing against private clubs, he was a member of the Garrick in London, but he felt the social pretensions of Americans to be somewhat absurd. He'd heard of the Avenue Club, but he hardly thought of membership as a great mark of distinction.

"Okay," said Cecil, "Let's pretend you're right. It's the best club in New York. So what? The Avenue doesn't strike me as your kind of place."

Max scowled furiously.

"Why is that? I'm not sophisticated enough? Too unrefined?"

"No," said Cecil, "I just don't think you'd like it there."

"I'll decide what I like, you little shit. You think I should be content to be a guest in the club dining room. I'm lucky if I can steal a matchbook from the bar."

"Not what I said."

Max reached over and squeezed Cecil's fingers.

"I know what you said, even if you didn't say it. It's written all over your face, and let me tell you something young man, the only difference between Max Guberstein and the Prince of Wales, the Prince gets out of the shower to piss."

"Do you have friends at the Avenue club?" asked Cecil blandly.

"In fact, I have a number of friends at the club. My banker's a member, my lawyer's a member, and if I had a fucking therapist he'd probably be a member too."

"And you're considering joining yourself?"

"Correct, Mr. Biddle," Max took a breath. "And you are going to help me get in. That's your project."

"You might as well ask me to grow bananas in Central Park." Cecil tried to remain calm but he was unnerved. Bananas in Central Park might be easier. "It's not like joining a gym, Max. You don't just walk in and write a check. The process takes months."

"I understand what's involved, thank you. Recommendations, lunches, cocktails. I'm not asking you to start from scratch. I've already done most of the work. The spring elections are just eight days away."

"Then how can I possibly help?"

"I've run into a snag," said Max. "Let me explain. My election to the club will be decided by the people on the admissions committee, so it's important for me to know what they're thinking. Until very recently I could rely on a young man named Jos Nicols to keep me informed, but Mr. Nicols has been sent to Tokyo and he no longer sits on the committee."

"You want me to kidnap Jos Nicols and drag him back to New York?"

"Shut up," said Max. "I want to you to talk to Mr. Nicols' replacement on the committee. It turns out he's a friend of yours."

"Who?"

"Dante Penfield."

"Dante? Are you sure? He is a friend of mine but he's not the kind of person who gets put on admissions committees. Certainly not at the Avenue Club."

"I don't mind," said Max, "arguing about matters of opinion, but I don't like to be challenged on matters of fact. Dante Penfield is on the admissions committee. I found out last night. I need his help and I need you to make sure I get it. Do you understand?"

"Yes, sorry, understood." Cecil saw there was no way out and resigned himself to the assignment. "What sort of help are we looking for?"

Max sketched out the details.

The admissions process at the Avenue Club was an arduous affair, and it really did go on for months. First you got a member to put you up, then you had to find someone else to second you. Then there were letters of recommendation to collect, fourteen in all, followed by drinks parties and a number of tête-à-tête meetings with various members. You had to make nice with everyone, but it was the men on the admissions committee who mattered most because they were the only people who actually voted. There were seven men on the admissions committee and their vote had to be unanimous. Max had made a study of each one of them, and drawing heavily on conversations he'd had with the departed Jos Nicols, his analysis was as follows:

John Newbury was the most inconsequential member of the admissions committee. Max called him Happy Boy and he was a genial fellow who'd never met a man he didn't like. He could be relied upon to vote in Max's favor because he always voted in favor. Next there was old Mr. Sears. Sears wasn't a natural ally, but he liked people who were useful and Max had performed a significant service for his daughter. Max had confidence in Sears. Then there was Ben Jentsen, whom Max described contemptuously as a bleeding heart. Jentsen was solidly in Max's camp because he believed in broadening the club's membership, and he supported the candidacy of all Jews on principle.

But after Jentsen, the picture got muddier. Tad Wainwright was the quintessential Avenue Club man. He was an American version of the retired English Colonel in a drawing room comedy. Wainwright was Groton and Harvard. He cared desperately about what he called *a man's bona fides*, and when he met Max for dinner the first question out of his mouth was, "Where did you prep?" Wainwright was a potential problem but he wasn't an independent thinker, and Max figured that if a consensus developed, Wainwright would roll over. But how to develop a consensus?

The twin keys were Puff Penfield, the club President, and Dick Burkus the head of the admissions committee. Puff didn't sit on the committee himself but he had a proxy in Mr. Bullard (Dante's former employer) who represented his interests. Max was fairly certain of Puff and Mr. Bullard, but he was nervous about Dick Burkus, and in any case, he wanted to keep watch on all three. Max reiterated:

"So really it comes down to two people, Puff Penfield and Dick Burkus. If I can get them, I'll get the rest. I think I have Puff, but I'm less sure of Dick, and what I need from you," Max stared hard at Cecil, "Is to tell your friend Dante to keep his eyes open at the committee meeting this week. I want to know what happens and what people are saying about me. You better tell him to vote for me, too. The elections are in a week's time and it's your job to make sure I don't get turned down."

"You mean blackballed," said Cecil. "People don't get turned down at the Avenue Club, the word is blackballed. They vote by putting marbles in a cigar box. A black marble means you don't get in."

"I know the terminology," said Max sharply. "I don't use it because I think it's infantile. *Blackballed.*"

After a pause Cecil said: "May I ask you a question, Max?"

"What?"

"Why do you want to join the Avenue Club?"

"Mind your own business."

"Not even a hint?"

Max closed his eyes for a moment.

"Let's just say I'm doing an old friend a favor. Don't ask me again."

Cecil didn't press and he finished his breakfast in silence. Considering this latest task, Cecil asked himself how he might be of use in getting Max elected to the club. Nothing came immediately to mind. It was not as though one could bribe one's way in. Despite Max's belief that money is catnip, there are some things that cannot be bought. Men like Dick Burkus have money enough already and they tend to live by caprice. It was hard to imagine how his arm might be twisted.

"Is there anything else I have to do today?" asked Cecil.

"First we've got the Navy Yard investors," said Max. He wanted to turn part of the old Brooklyn Navy Yard into a film studio. "We're meeting here, then driving out to Brooklyn. Afterwards I'm coming back to the hotel for a nap, but I want you to go out to Coney Island and visit Mrs. Schuler. It's her birthday so bring some flowers and give her a nice hour. Tonight you're going to the theatre. Penfield's daughter is in a show called *Room 421*. I want you to make nice."

Cecil listened absentmindedly. He wondered whether Penelope had telephoned after he'd left the hotel. He hoped she hadn't. She didn't always believe in his early morning meetings. He went outside to smoke another cigarette before the Navy Yard investors arrived.

There were three people in the party of Navy Yard investors, two principles and a lawyer. Max talked to them for half an hour in the dining room of the Pierre, and afterwards they went out to the street where two limousines were waiting to take them to Brooklyn.

Old Money

Max and Cecil took one limousine while the two principles took the other. The lawyer didn't know what to do. He tried squeezing in with his investors but he was shooed away and at the last minute the lawyer jumped into the front seat of Max's limousine. Max ordered the driver to stop and screamed at the top of his lungs:

"My view! You're blocking my view!"

The lawyer got out and the limousines rolled off. Cecil looked back through the rear window and saw the lawyer running down the street, frantically hailing a cab. Cecil said to Max:

"You're an awful man."

Max didn't flinch.

"He was blocking my view. Now sit up straight and try not to move."

Cecil did as he was told and Max slumped over on his shoulder and fell fast asleep.

6

Mrs. Schuler, first name Lenore, whom it was Cecil's job to visit that afternoon, was a widow who lived in Coney Island. Cecil had met her once before at a dinner celebrating Max's lifetime achievement in film. Mrs. Schuler had made a short toast. She introduced herself as Max's kindergarten teacher and a close friend to his mother before she died, and she went on to say that Max had always been a sweet natured boy and very considerate of others. Cecil wasn't so sure about that, but perhaps it was true as Mrs. Schuler saw it. Max did seem to go out of his way for her. Certainly, she was the only person from his childhood with whom he kept in touch.

After some difficulty finding the right house, Cecil rang the door bell and Lenore answered wearing a polyester house dress. Her gray hair was tinted purple and she had a pair of glasses on a chain around her neck. Cecil explained that he worked for Max and that he had come to wish her a happy birthday. Then he apologized for Max's absence, saying that Max had been called back to Manhattan at the last minute for an urgent meeting. Lenore didn't appear to care one way or the other and she invited Cecil in for a glass of water.

Cecil had bought a floral arrangement at the bodega around the corner, and handing it to Lenore, he pointed out the card that came with it. Lenore put on her glasses to read:

To the most wonderful teacher in the world. Best wishes on this special day from your loving friend, Max.

Hearing the words out loud Cecil worried that he might have overdone it with the handwritten note, but at least there was no danger of Lenore noticing it wasn't Max's penmanship. Because Max never used pens. Cecil couldn't recall ever having seen him hold one.

"Such a considerate boy," said Lenore. It was unclear which boy, Max or Cecil, she had in mind, but she put the flowers in a vase and told Cecil to take a seat on the sofa. "Nice weather today."

"Very nice. Don't you love spring?"

Lenore didn't answer and Cecil shifted anxiously in his seat, searching for another topic of conversation. Every old woman he knew liked to talk about gardening, so he decided to milk the birthday bouquet a bit longer.

"Beautiful isn't it? I wish I knew more about these things." Cecil was doing his inquisitive student impression. "Can you tell me what the pink ones are? I think they're tulips but perhaps they're carnations. And the yellow ones are daisies, isn't that right?"

"I don't know from flowers," said Lenore.

She shrugged and fell silent again, and after this second setback Cecil began to think it was going to be a very long hour indeed. He should have had more faith, however, because it turned out that Lenore was quite capable of leading the discussion herself, and she was just waiting for Cecil to cede the floor. Once he stopped talking, she had plenty to say. She spoke about her gout and her arthritis; she spoke about a peculiar stomach disorder for which she had coined the term "lower gassiness"; she spoke about the second war and her uncle who died in it; and when at last she got up from her chair, it wasn't to say goodbye, but only to fetch an old photo album to look through.

The hour quickly became ninety minutes and Cecil's face grew tired from smiling. When his buttocks went numb it was time to leave, but Lenore wouldn't let him go empty handed. She gave him a picture to take back to Max. It was one of the photos from her album that had come unstuck, and since she couldn't be bothered to glue it back in, she asked him to pass it on as a keepsake.

"I'll make sure he gets it," said Cecil.

He kissed Mrs. Schuler on both cheeks then hurried out to catch a taxi back to Manhattan. It was getting late and Cecil still had to track down Dante to discuss next week's election at the Avenue Club.

Telling the doorman he was expected, Cecil let himself in to Dante's empty apartment on 89th Street. He poured himself a glass of sherry, slipped off his shoes and lay down on the sofa, waiting for Dante to come home. He stared blankly at the ceiling for ten minutes, before reaching into his pocket and taking out the photograph Lenore had given him. It was a curious picture, a small black and white of Max's family standing together under an awning on Fifth Avenue in the 1960's. Max looked to be about eighteen years old, and he was sandwiched between his mother on one side and a much younger girl, presumably his sister, on the other. Max's father stood behind them and it must have been raining because he was holding an umbrella over his wife's head. It didn't seem like much fun. Max's sister was smiling, but the rest of them stared at the camera as if waiting for a funeral procession to pass.

"What are you doing here?" said Dante.

"Oh, hey." Cecil sat up. "I hope you don't mind I let myself in. I know you keep the front door unlocked."

"Saves me from forgetting my keys," said Dante. "What are you drinking?"

"Sherry. Very good sherry, in fact. Where'd you get it?"

"It's a present from mother. She's still sending me a case every year. I used to love it but I've lost the taste a bit. No one drinks sherry anymore. People call it a woman's drink."

"Yes, I've heard that too. It's rubbish. The best thing is not to pay any attention and do as you please. No one ever notices."

"What've you got in your hand?" asked Dante.

Cecil gave him the photograph.

"Who are they?"

"It's Max Guberstein and his family. His kindergarten teacher gave it to me."

"They all look wretched," said Dante, "Except the girl. Who's she?"

"I don't know. Max's sister, I suppose. It's odd to think he has a sister. I've never heard him mention her. She's probably married to a dentist in New Jersey and they don't speak."

"She's pretty."

"Was pretty," said Cecil. He was feeling philosophical. "She'd be at least fifty by now and women lose their looks. My father once told me a story about old Lady Cartwright who used to cry whenever she saw a beautiful girl. She said it was like looking at a lush green hillside just before the strip miners moved in. Apparently Lady Cartwright was gorgeous when she was younger and it always upset her to be reminded of what she'd lost."

Dante stared at the pretty young girl in the picture and tried to imagine what she would look like as a woman of fifty. He couldn't tell.

"Wait a minute," said Dante. "Did you notice the awning? That's 740 5th Avenue. It's where Uncle Puff lives. Do you think Max grew up in that building?"

"Not even close. Max is from Coney Island. I just came from there. Block after block of row houses with the elevated tracks running right through the middle of everything. It sounds like thunder when the train goes past."

"Then why the picture?"

"It must've been taken on some ghastly family outing," said Cecil. "You know, a trip to Manhattan to show the children how the other half lives. I imagine a visit to the museum and plates of cold tongue at a deli. No wonder they all look miserable."

"Except the sister."

"Well yes, except her."

Cecil put the photograph back in his pocket and stood up to get himself another sherry. He poured a glass for Dante too.

"Last night Audrey said she might be leaving New York. Do you think she's serious?"

"Yes, I do."

"Aren't you upset about it?"

"Of course, I'm upset," said Dante. "I think it's awful. She wants to move to Iowa."

"Why Iowa?"

"Money. She needs her doctorate and the University of Iowa is offering a bigger stipend than she can get here."

"How much bigger?"

"$10,000 a year. Over five years it's quite a lot."

"Couldn't your mother make up the difference?"

"She could, but Audrey would never accept it. I wouldn't even know how to make the suggestion."

"Then what are you going to do?"

"There's nothing I can do, I just keep hoping something will come up to change her mind. At least she doesn't have to decide for another two months."

"The worst is not," said Cecil, "So long as you can say, this is worst."

"What's that?"

"Shakespeare, I think. I like the sound of it."

"I don't see how it fits with Audrey moving to Iowa."

"Maybe it doesn't."

"Then let's change the subject," said Dante, "It's too depressing. What are you up to?"

"Pure cat piss," said Cecil.

"What's wrong?"

"Oh, everything. My life is a mess, Dante. But look, I really need your help with something. It's about Max."

"Max? I doubt I'll be much use. You know, I met him in the flesh yesterday. I don't think I made a good impression."

"Nobody does."

"He was at Uncle Puff's in Long Island for Trixie's Africa party. During the speeches she called him a true lover of wildlife. I wouldn't have picked him for that."

"He's not."

"But Trixie thanked him especially. He must have given a pile of money to her elephants."

"I'm sure he did, but it wasn't to pay for a park in Africa. Max was there to butter up your Uncle Puff."

"I'm not sure Puff is butterable."

"Possibly not, but that's the way Max thinks. Grease the wheels."

"How does Puff come into it?"

"Because he's president of the Avenue Club and Max is up for election a week from tomorrow."

"Yes, that's right," said Dante. "Mr. Bullard told me. It's rather odd, don't you think. Why would Max want to join the Avenue Club?"

Cecil threw up his hands: "He says he's doing it as a favor to a friend, but that makes no sense. I have no idea what his real motives are. Maybe he's planning to take up squash, but I suspect it's more about small town, pecking order stuff. Max has a chip on his shoulder. He hates the Avenue crowd, but he runs into them all the time in the money world, and he probably thinks they're sneering at him, which pisses him off. I bet he wants to join the club just to rub their noses in it, just to prove he can. At least that's my guess, but you never know with Max, and it doesn't really matter anyway. The key point is he wants to join and he's assigned me to make sure he gets in."

"Then you're in luck," said Dante, "I've just been put on the admissions committee."

"I know, Max told me. He also said you have a meeting tomorrow night, the last one before the election. I need a favor, Dante. I need you to keep track of everything that happens at the meeting so I can make a report back to Max. Do you mind? I have to do whatever I can. If Max doesn't get into the club, he's gonna have to blame somebody and I'm fairly certain he's going to blame me."

"That's hardly reasonable," said Dante.

"No, it's not, but there you are."

Cecil went on to explain the precariousness of his relationship with Max and the delicate status of his employment. Cecil was soon to get fired, but he needed Max's help in order to get another job and he couldn't afford to end up on the black list.

"If Max doesn't get into the Avenue Club, he'll kill my chances at SouthEnd Pictures and I'll be out of work. I won't be able to stay in America. I'll have to go back to London."

Cecil paused to let the significance of these last words sink in.

"But if you went back to London," said Dante, putting the pieces together, "You'd have to move in with Penelope."

"That's right."

"You'd have no excuse not to get married."

"None at all."

"Can't you break off the engagement?"

"She'd claw my eyes out."

"Yes, I think she would."

"So you'll help me with the club?"

"I will," said Dante, "But I wouldn't make too much of our chances. I'd say it's an uphill battle. There aren't a lot of movie producers in the Avenue. Not a lot of Gubersteins either."

"I agree, but there's got to be a first time for everything, and if Max thinks it's worth a try I have to believe him. He's not one for tilting at windmills."

"What has he told you so far?"

"Max described it as chiefly a matter of lining up your Uncle Puff with someone named Dick Burkus."

"Head of the admissions committee," said Dante. "Max is probably right, but it won't be easy lining them up. Puff and Dick are on bad terms at the moment. If either one pushes too hard in one direction, the other might push back just out of cussedness."

"Hmmm, Max didn't mention. Maybe that's what's behind his difficulty with Dick. For some reason Max thinks he's got Puff in the bag, but Dick seems to be immune to his charm."

"Dick is immune to a lot of people's charm."

"That may be, but you've still got to let me know what he says at the meeting tomorrow night. Okay?" Dante nodded and Cecil now felt free to move on to pleasanter subjects. "Audrey tells me you've written a screenplay."

"I have, *The Darkness of Daisy's Back Passage*."

"What's it about?"

Dante launched into a long synopsis of the plot. Daisy, Caleb Astor, the game of *I Never*. Cecil did his best to feign interest.

"Do you want to read it?"

"Maybe later."

"Oh."

"Don't take it badly," said Cecil. "I'm very busy at the moment, but if everything works out with the Avenue Club, I promise to read it right away. I could even get Max to buy the rights."

"Really?"

"Sure."

"How much would he pay?"

"Can't say exactly, but enough to make it worth your while."

Dante was immediately taken with the idea of selling his screenplay to Max and he imagined sitting on set in a canvas chair shouting out stage directions through a megaphone: Feeling! Energy! Take two!

The front door opened. Audrey was home and she dropped her bags down on the floor with a thud.

"Hello boys. You want to know what I've been doing all day? Not that you asked, but I spent the whole afternoon looking for a single book, *The Senior Commoner* by Julian Hall. Phillip Larkin talks about it in one of his essays. He used to read it whenever he felt depressed. But it's not in any of the New York libraries and I just wasted two hours searching on the internet. Gone without a trace. It's rather sad in a way, a reminder of mortality. It's amazing to think of how much effort gets put into all the books no one ever gets the chance to read. It's like the writers are just wasting their time. Anyway, I wish I could get hold of Hall's novel. It'd be interesting to know how a man like Larkin cheered himself up."

Audrey's story got no response and she suddenly became aware of having interrupted something.

"What have you two been up to?" she asked. "You look like you've been plotting to overthrow the government."

Dante laughed. "Business, business. Max Guberstein is going to buy my screenplay."

"But only after he gets into the Avenue Club," Cecil added.

"Wonderful," said Audrey. "You can fill me in over dinner. You are taking us out to dinner, aren't you Cecil?"

"Of course."

Audrey put a hand on Dante's shoulder. "Listen, there's something I need to tell you. Your mother phoned yesterday. She said she's coming to New York."

Dante flinched, "When?"

"Soon. She didn't say precisely, but in the next few days. She told me she has business in the city, but there may be more to it than that. I think she's back on one of her mother worry kicks."

"And quite right," said Cecil grinning. "I'm worried too. Poor Dante, all by himself. Do you know, I've known Dante all my life and I've never once seen him with a girlfriend?"

"Don't tease," said Audrey firmly.

"No, I'm quite used to it," said Dante, whose sex life, or absence of one, was a long standing fascination of Cecil's.

"You're not gay, are you?" asked Cecil.

"Not that I know of."

"But you can't be certain, can you? I once heard an interview with a man who said he didn't find out he was gay until he was forty-five. You're not even thirty."

"Yes, well it's a pity there's not a test I can take to find out right away."

"Maybe there is," Cecil replied. "Did you suffer much from constipation as a boy?"

"What's that got to do with it?" asked Audrey.

"A little theory I'm developing. I believe gay men are more likely to suffer constipation as children."

"Where did you get that?"

"A friend of mine. He told me he was always constipated until he came out of the closet. Then I read about a similar case in a magazine article."

"Is it just men or does it work for gay women too?" asked Audrey.

"I couldn't say, I don't know many lesbians. In any case, I don't know why you want to group them together. Gay men have nothing to do with lesbians, they're much more like straight men than anything else. They're just straight men who like boys instead of girls."

"I hope you know how stupid you sound," said Audrey.

"It's only a theory," Cecil replied.

"Then tell me about dinner instead. Where are you taking us?"

"Your choice," said Cecil grandly, "Compliments of GoldStream Pictures. And after dinner we're going to a show."

"What sort of show?"

"A searing portrayal of the human passions, I'm sure. Joy and sadness mixed in equal proportions. You'll laugh, you'll cry, and you'll see Cat Penfield as you've never seen her before."

"Cat?" said Dante. "Is this something Max put you up to?"

"We shall leave no stone unturned. C'mon let's go."

7

The Progressive Arts Theater was on 6th Street between First Avenue and Avenue A. You couldn't tell it was a theater from the outside. It looked more like a warehouse than anything else. There was no marquee, only a gray steel door with a xeroxed flyer taped up announcing tonight's show, *Room 421: Scenes From Life*.

Cecil insisted on looking for seats in the back. He had been on a number of scouting missions to places like the Progressive Arts Theater, he knew there was a risk of falling asleep, and he didn't like to offend the actors. Dante and Audrey wanted to sit in the back as well, because they were both secretly worried that the sight of Cat Penfield onstage might bring on a violent case of the giggles.

Unfortunately, the theater was too small to offer much protection. There was no raised stage or raked seating. It was just a big, brightly lit, rectangular room with three rows of folding chairs laid out along one side. Cecil muttered something under his breath and led the way to the far corner of the room. They found chairs by the window, and while Cecil chatted with Audrey, Dante studied the house.

There were roughly forty people in the audience and it was a modish crowd. One man had a pierced lip, another a pierced eyebrow, and the girl in front of Dante had a shaved head and an interesting snake tattoo running down the small of her back into her butt crack. He couldn't see where the snake's head ended up but he caught a glimpse of the tail whenever she leant forward.

Judging by their looks, Dante guessed most of the audience was made up of other actors, but there were two people that stood out distinctly from the rest, a well dressed elderly couple sitting stiffly together right in the middle of the front row. The woman wore a white blouse and diamond earrings, and she was smiling. The man wore a dark gray suit, and his jaw was clenched so tight he might have been wearing a muzzle. It was Trixie and Puff, and the sight of them put butterflies in Dante's tummy. He nudged Audrey on the elbow to point them out.

According to Dante's program, the show lasted seventy minutes. Like the soul of St. Augustine, it was a work in progress, and it consisted of three different scenes each of which had been developed by the actors themselves as part of an ongoing process. Dante scanned the names to find which scene Cat was in, and he had just time to see that she came last when the house lights cut out and the room went dark.

When the lights came back on, two young actors, a man and a woman, had taken their places in the center of the room. The woman sat on a sofa and the man stood over to one side looking out an imaginary window. The set up was a rainy Saturday morning in the couple's apartment and you could tell right away they were itching for a fight. It started with the woman complaining about her emotional isolation, it turned briefly to the subject of the man's sexual frustration, and then it settled into a long argument about an upcoming visit from the man's ex-girlfriend. Finally the woman started to cry and the scene whimpered to a close:

Man: Shit, I'm sorry. I'm not trying to hurt you.
Woman: Do you want to just end it?
Man: I don't know. Do you?
Woman: No, not yet.
Man: Me neither.
Woman: Hey, is it still raining?
Man (staring out the window): Yeah.

The house lights flickered, and two new actors appeared on stage. The second scene was similar to the first except that the second girl was prettier and this time she was the one upset about not having enough sex. There was a long screaming match, then the girl started crying, and she sobbed through almost a full minute before delivering the last line:

Woman: So this is love?

There was silence and the house went dark again. Cecil, who had been resting his eyes, sat up and looked sharp. Even Audrey felt a small thrill run up her spine, and Dante could hardly contain his excitement as the lights came back on and Cat Penfield walked out to take the stage. Cat was almost unrecognizable. She was dressed in ripped jeans and a baggy t-shirt. She wasn't wearing a bra, so her large breasts bounced around freely when she moved. She had dark smears of mascara around her eyes and her long blonde hair looked as though it hadn't seen a brush in weeks.

The actor who played Cat's boyfriend was a fat young man in a ski hat, and they stood facing each other in front of the sofa with venom in their eyes. The man gestured to speak, but Cat wouldn't let him. She slammed her fist into her palm, and in her sweet, girlish voice, she sang out the first line:

Cat: God damn it!
Man: What the fuck is your problem?
Cat: It's not my fucking problem! It's your fucking problem!

Dante wondered if Puff, who abhorred bad language, had ever heard his daughter curse before, and he stole a look at him in the front row. But if Puff was upset he wasn't showing it. He was sitting exactly as before, rigid and emotionless, with his jaw clenched tight. You had to admire his stoicism.

As the scene progressed, it turned out Cat was pregnant. Her boyfriend wanted her to have an abortion but she wouldn't agree to it, and for twenty minutes they acted out a furious spat. Then at the end there was a twist and Cat said she wasn't pregnant after all, she was only pretending in order to test her boyfriend's love:

Cat: And you failed the fucking test!

Man: You're right, honey. I failed. I'm sorry.

Cat: That's all you can say?

Man: That's all I can say. I love you and I failed.

The actors from all three scenes came out for a bow and there was a big round of applause. Dante pronounced it the best night of theater he'd seen in years, but Cecil was more circumspect and in response to Audrey's raised eyebrow he answered pensively, "Cat's got nice tits."

After the show the cast and their friends gathered at a bar down the street. Puff and Trixie went too. Trixie liked meeting young people because it made her feel young herself, and she dragged Cat around the bar eager to meet everyone she could. Puff was less eager. He felt out of place. At least at the theater there was somewhere to sit, but standing at the bar, vainly trying to order a drink, Puff got a nasty sense that the young people were laughing at him.

"Dante!" Puff exclaimed, enormously relieved at the sight of a familiar face.

"Hello Puff," said Dante.

"Hi Puff," said Audrey.

Puff shook Dante's hand but looked right through Audrey. He'd met her a number of times, but he could never remember who she was. He knew she had something to do with Dante's apartment, but she wasn't a girlfriend, and all Puff could think was that perhaps she was the housekeeper. What Puff couldn't understand was why Dante would be going out at night with his housekeeper.

"Did you like the play?" asked Dante, breaking the momentary silence. "I thought Cat was great."

"Don't be an idiot. I'm trying to get myself a drink."

Cecil stepped in, gestured to the bartender and bought the first round.

"Who's are you?" asked Puff.

"Cecil Biddle. Nice to meet you Puff."

"He's an old friend," said Dante.

"Sshhh," said Puff. "Biddle, you say? The Philadelphia Biddle's? Let's see, I went to college with George, class of '57, he became a doctor and summers in Blue Hill. Also there was his brother Barton Biddle, class of '59. I don't know what Barton does."

"Distant cousins. I'm afraid I've never met them."

"Hmphh." In the game of *Small World* distant cousins don't count for much. Puff tried again. "You've got an accent. Where are you from?"

"London."

"Alright then, we're getting somewhere. There was a Peter Biddle I used to know years ago. Lived in Kensington and ran a shipping company, very attractive wife. Thomasin I think her name was. Peter's probably sixty by now."

"Dark hair?"

"Yes," said Puff, "That's him."

"Remarkable," said Cecil, "My uncle Peter."

Cecil didn't have any uncles but he'd played *Small World* enough that he knew what it meant to men like Puff.

"Do you see him much?"

"Not since I was a boy."

"Pity, I'd like to know how he's doing. I haven't thought about Peter Biddle in ages. Imagine running into his nephew at a bar like this."

It wasn't a complete victory, but the foreign angle was worth a few extra points and Puff blew the whistle, uttering the phrase that brought the game to an official close.

"Small world, isn't it?"

"A small world," said Cecil philosophically.

"Small bladder," said Audrey, doing her best to imitate Cecil's tone. Puff gave her a funny look, and she skipped away while Dante led the discussion back to *Room 421*.

"I don't understand the fascination with four-letter words," said Puff. "Every line was *bleep* this or *bleep* that. It's sheer laziness if you ask me. These writers nowadays would rather scream obscenities than tell you something interesting. It's because they have nothing to say. What a waste of time."

"I disagree," said Cecil, "Putting aside the bad language, I thought it was an excellent show. Cat's performance in particular. She's a very talented actress."

"How would you know?"

"I study actors for a living."

"What does that mean?"

"I'm a movie producer. I work for Max Guberstein."

"Max?"

If it had been anyone else, Puff would have taken the opportunity to comment once more on the delightful smallness of the world. Instead he just looked surprised.

"Did Max tell you to come to the play tonight?"

"Yes, he met Cat at your house on Long Island a few days ago and he was quite taken with her. I can see why. She's got a real chance to make a career for herself."

"As an actress?"

"Max wants me to help her find an agent. Then she can start getting cast. Here, let me give you my card."

Cecil reached into his jacket pocket and as he pulled out his wallet, the photograph Mrs. Shuler had given him fell out and fluttered to the floor. Puff reached down to pick it up.

"Who are these people?"

"That's Max and his family," said Cecil.

Puff brought the picture right up to his nose and studied it more closely. "Look, they're standing outside 740. That's my building." Puff continued staring at the photograph for another minute. "May I ask a favor? Do you think Max would mind if I held on to this for a few days?"

"Be my guest. You can keep it if you like."

"No need," said Puff.

He put the photograph away just as Trixie and Cat joined the group, and Audrey returned from the bathroom. Audrey squeezed in next to Dante and congratulated Cat on her performance.

"Thanks!" said Cat.

Cecil introduced himself. He kissed Trixie on both cheeks, then turned his attention to Cat, looking her up and down admiringly. Drawing Cat aside, Cecil explained that he worked for Max and wanted to help her find an agent. Audrey rolled her eyes and pulled gently on Dante's sleeve, realizing it was the end of their night with Cecil.

Old Money

"Well, I think we're off," said Dante.

"Us too," Puff replied. "Come on Trixie, come on Cat."

"Not yet Daddy," said Cat pleadingly.

Cecil put on his serious face. "If you don't mind, I'd like a few minutes with Cat to discuss the business."

"Of course," said Trixie. "Come along, Puff. Let's let them enjoy themselves."

After the others had gone, Cecil and Cat remained together at the bar.

"You're a wonderful actress."

"Honest? You think so?"

Cecil laid his left hand, the one with the missing finger, gently on Cat's forearm to reassure her of his sincerity.

"Hey," she said, "How did you lose your pinkie?"

It was a long story.

"What are you doing? Let me in. Let me in!"

As Dante and Audrey walked down 6th Street towards the subway they saw an elderly gentleman struggling with a giant bouncer who was standing guard outside a run down bar.

"One more drink, just one more," said the man.

"Go home," said the bouncer.

The old man took a step away from the door as if to leave, then surged suddenly forward. He thrust his two hands into the bouncer's stomach and pushed with all his might. The bouncer didn't budge. He calmly turned the drunk around, lifted him by the armpits and dragged him away from the bar entrance, dropping him on a stoop down the street.

"Where do you live?" asked the bouncer, "I'll get you a taxi."

The old man didn't respond and the bouncer went back to his doorway. Now the old man put his head in his hands and made a strange baying noise. Dante and Audrey stopped and stared.

Noticing them, the old man raised his head and straightened his back. He wasn't an ordinary drunk. He reminded Audrey of Peter O'Toole in *My Favorite Year*. He wore a blue pinstriped suit, a crisp white shirt and a red silk tie. He had a good pair of shoes on his feet and his thick gray hair was neatly parted to the side. His face was weathered with age but he still had fine features and all the gin in his belly gave his cheeks a rosy glow.

"It's Tweedle!" said Dante.

"Sshhh, Dante, sshhh. I need to talk to this young lady." Tweedle held out his hand to Audrey. "Young lady can you help me? I've had too much to drink and I need to get home."

"Where do you live?" she asked.

"That's part of the problem. I can't remember. I know I live on the upper east side, but I seem to have forgotten the exact address. Perhaps if you could help me find my wallet, I believe it contains my card." Tweedle smiled sheepishly and tried to look gallant but he was overcome by the effort and slumped forward into a ball.

"Who is he?" said Audrey.

"Tweedle Barnes. He's a member of the Avenue Club. He's the ball bearer."

"Ball bearer?" Audrey shook her head.

"It's sort of an honorary position. The ball bearer carries the ballot box from the admissions committee to the President's lounge on election night. I think Tweedle does it for the free whiskey. He's rather eccentric but he's a nice man. What are we going to do with him?"

"We can't leave him on the sidewalk," said Audrey. Tweedle was still slumped over in a ball. "You hold up his shoulders and I'll see if I can find his wallet."

Searching Tweedle's pockets Audrey found a total of twenty-three dollars scattered about his person. She also found his keys, a packet of breath mints, and a map of the Mount Katahdin Baxter State Park in Maine. Finally she found his wallet. Tweedle's card said he lived on 81st Street between 1st and 2nd. Dante shook him by the shoulders.

"Come on Tweedle, wake up."

"You live on 81st Street," said Audrey.

"That's right," said Tweedle.

"Can you get home by yourself?"

Tweedle paused. "No, I don't think I can."

Dante hailed a cab and they all three rode uptown together.

"See that place?" said Tweedle. They were standing on 81st Street outside Tweedle's apartment. The struggle to get Tweedle out of the cab had brought him around a bit and he was pointing to the building next to his. "That place is a brothel. The sign says it's a law office but it's not. I can hear them through my wall. Men going in and out of there all night long, and in the morning you see the girls leaving. I've never been to a brothel myself."

Tweedle climbed his stoop and tried opening the front door, but fumbling with his keys, he couldn't get the lock to turn. Tweedle was more sober than he'd been half an hour ago, he'd recovered his head, but he was still having trouble with his arms and legs. Audrey took charge of the keys and opened the door.

"Fourth floor," said Tweedle. There was no elevator so Dante had to push him up the stairs. "Apartment on the left."

Audrey unlocked the door and Tweedle staggered across to his bed.

"Oh," said Dante.

Tweedle's apartment was not more than fifteen foot square and the single window looked out onto a ventilation shaft. Apart from a narrow bed there were only two pieces of furniture in the entire room. One was a plain wooden chair with a stack of old gardening magazines piled on it, the other was a small bookcase. Tweedle had a bathroom but no kitchen, and although there was a small closet to hang up suits and shirts, there was no bureau for underwear or socks, and these were arranged in piles on the floor at the foot of the bed. The paint on the walls was peeling, much of the plaster was cracked, and when Dante turned on the light switch, it was only a bare bulb that hung from the ceiling.

Tweedle lay on top of his dirty gray sheets and crossed his hands over his chest. Audrey lifted his head and slipped a pillow underneath it.

"You're not leaving are you?" said Tweedle. Now that he was lying down he felt much better. "It's very nice of you to take me home. Can't you stay a few minutes?"

Audrey patted his hands and sat down on the bed beside him. Dante moved the gardening magazines and sat on the chair.

"Do you know what I was thinking just now?" said Tweedle, "I was thinking how lucky the two of you are. You're young. Youth is the greatest thing anyone can have. I miss it. I miss the pleasure of life. I think the capacity for joy decreases as you get older. Every day you lose a bit of happiness."

While Tweedle talked Dante browsed the titles in his bookcase. Most of the books were about botany, but they were mixed in with a lot of schoolboy stories. There was a copy of *Tom Brown's School Days* next to a book on roses; Cyril Connolly's *Enemies of Promise* was jammed up against *Soil, Mulch & You.*

Tweedle stared up at the ceiling and continued wistfully:

"I'll give you an example. I've been drinking most of my life and when I was eighteen there was nothing I liked better than a spree. There used to be real excitement in a bottle of gin. But twenty years later I was still drinking and the excitement wasn't the same; it was just a way to stave off boredom. Now I've been drinking for almost fifty years and I can't see anything in it at all. Alcohol just makes me depressed."

"Why don't you stop?" said Audrey.

"Habit I suppose. Maybe I should stop. But I get lonely sometimes. Don't you ever get lonely?"

"Not really," said Audrey.

"You're lucky, then. I get very lonely sometimes. I've always thought it would be nice to have a companion. You know, someone to share my life with. Friendship, tenderness, comfort from the howling winds. Of course, there are probably drawbacks to living with someone else, but I wouldn't know."

"You've never had a girlfriend?" asked Audrey.

"No, I haven't. Very little of that for me. Not that I wasn't curious, but I hadn't the drive to see it through. With women you need drive and boldness, two things I lack. I've always been slightly afraid of women. I used to get urges all the time, I still do on occasion, but my libido was never strong enough to conquer my fear. So I always ended up by myself. Usually with a drink in my hand and a book on my lap. Boils down to being shy."

"You don't seem shy to me," said Audrey.

"I'm shy with women, at least the ones I'm interested in. I don't know why. It's just the way I am. You'd think I come from a very prudish family, but I don't."

Tweedle recalled a long forgotten story from his youth and laughed. "Do you mind if I tell you a story? It's slightly off-color."

"Go ahead," said Audrey.

Dante wasn't listening. He'd made a discovery in the bookcase. He'd found a book called *The Senior Commoner* by Julian Hall, and he was trying to remember why the title sounded familiar. Tweedle went on:

"There was a boy I went to college with and our families used to summer together in Maine. He was a notorious swordsman and he came down with a case of VD. All of us knew about it. I was at a garden party one summer and a group of us were talking about the boy's bad luck. We were speculating about who gave it to him. Probably a prostitute. In any case, my sister was at the garden party too. She was sixteen at the time, younger than me, and she overheard part of our conversation. In those days, we were more modest than people are now and VD wasn't something you talked about in mixed company. My sister went bright red in the face and ran away from the party without even saying goodbye. I ran after her and tried to apologize but she wouldn't talk to me. I thought she'd run away from the party because the conversation offended her. I felt quite guilty about it but then she started crying so I left her alone. Later I discovered that my sister wasn't nearly as innocent as I supposed. She wasn't offended by the conversation. She was upset because she had just slept with the swordsman. That's how she found out he had the clap and it turned out he'd given it to her as well. I had no idea."

Tweedle's mouth was dry and he smacked his lips together. Audrey asked if he'd like a glass of water.

"Yes, thank you. There should be a tumbler in the bathroom." Audrey got up to fetch the tumbler. Tweedle looked over at Dante.

"It's good of you to sit with me. I'm sorry about the surroundings."

"It's not so bad," said Dante.

Audrey gave Tweedle a glass of water and he drank it.

"Kind of you to say but you needn't be polite. I don't like it myself. I'll tell you what, I'd prefer to live in the country. I'd like to keep a garden and fill it with flowers and vegetables, perhaps a few fruit trees. Have you ever heard of W.H. Hudson? He was an English naturalist. He spent his time dreaming about plants and the open wilderness but he lived all his life in a squalid, dirty London street. It must have been torture for him. Sometimes I feel the same way. I'd like to get out of the city."

"Why don't you?" asked Dante.

"No money."

"But everyone at the club says you're swimming in it."

"Yes and it's quite decent of them really. It's their way of being friendly. It's not true."

"What about your inheritance?"

"There wasn't any. My mother left everything in trust. I get a small allowance but it's barely enough to cover the rent and my club dues."

Tweedle snuffled and yawned. He was nearing the end of his energies. He closed his eyes and started mumbling to himself. Perhaps he was thinking about his mother's house in Maine.

After Tweedle fell asleep Dante took his shoes off and loosened his tie. Audrey refilled his water glass and the two of them quietly left the apartment. They remained silent until they got back home.

8

Violet Penfield landed at JFK while Dante, Audrey and Cecil were still eating dinner. Although she'd made clear that a visit was pending, it was typical of her to leave the exact date of her arrival unannounced. Violet hated schedules and she objected to being tied down. She fancied she resembled Kierkegaard in this respect. If you were to invite Kierkegaard to dinner a week in advance he would thank you kindly but refuse to make a firm commitment on the grounds that 1) it is impossible to predict the future state of the world and 2) his own will power was not strong enough to hold to such promises as dinner a week from Tuesday. Violet admired that sort of thinking.

Traveling light, she sailed through customs and hurried out to catch a taxi to Manhattan. Violet had not been back to New York in two years, and driving along Park Avenue she looked up at the massive buildings in midtown and was reminded once more of the city's immense energy. Quite different from London. It was, she said, "like the difference between juice and concentrate." And this phrase, coming to her on the spur of the moment, pleased her so much that she made a mental note of it, intending to use it again.

"Yes thank you, up here on the right. The last awning. That's lovely. Now if you'll pop the trunk the doorman can get my case."

Violet took fifty dollars from her purse, paid the driver, and pointing the doorman to her suitcase, she glided into the building. Soon she was in Dante's apartment, her stockinged feet up on the sofa, drinking a mug of tea, and smoking a cigarette.

"Do you know what I like least about flying?" said Violet. She spoke out loud despite that she was alone in the room. Violet liked the sound of her own voice and she made a habit of talking to herself in private on the theory that it was good practice for when you had to talk to others in public. It taught you to speak with authority. She continued her soliloquy, "What I like least is that my feet swell up and I can never get my shoes back on when I land. What do you think causes the swelling? I'm told it's the cabin pressure." She took a long drag on her cigarette. "What I like second least is the nicotine depravation. All the airlines are non-smoking nowadays and it's devastating to one's well being. I must look a wreck."

Looking a wreck was one of Violet's commonest complaints and it wasn't false modesty. Whatever physical charms Dante possessed he got from his dead father not her. Violet was both shorter and rounder than she should be, and while she blamed her figure on her French boyfriend (a très good cook), it wasn't his fault that she was built like a bulldog, and it certainly wasn't his fault that she dressed as badly as she did.

Old Money

Violet liked tweed jackets on top of woolen trousers, and she made everything worse by wearing her hair in an appalling page boy cut which was much too young for her. The overall effect was so odd that she looked like a sinister ten year old boy, but Violet didn't give a fig what you thought of her appearance. She was impervious to comment.

She finished her tea, lit a second cigarette, and reviewed her plans.

Violet had come to New York for three reasons. The first of these was the most straightforward. Her Frenchman was bored with retirement and he wanted to open a new restaurant. Violet had agreed to finance the project and she intended to sell the cottage on Long Island to Puff in order to raise cash. Of course, the sale could have been managed from overseas, but it would go faster with Violet in New York and she needed the money sooner rather than later because Gascon had already signed his lease.

Violet picked up the phone and dialed her brother-in-law. The machine answered.

"Puff, it's Violet. I'm in New York and I'm selling the cottage. I assume you want to buy it but I'd like to get the thing done as quickly as possible. Let's think of a time to meet."

The second reason behind Violet's trip was a bit of a secret. It was an idea that had come to her only last week during a conversation with Cecil's mother in London, but the idea wasn't fully worked out yet and she wasn't certain how to discuss it, so she kept it to herlself.

The third reason that brought Violet to New York—"No," she corrected herself, "Not the third reason. In order of importance it's the first." — was because she loved her son. "Because I miss you, darling," said Violet, draining her tea and patting an imaginary Dante on his imaginary knee, "Because I'm worried about you and I want to make sure you're alright. I know you don't get to see me as often as you'd like, but you must realized that I am always thinking of you. Whatever it is Dante, you can always rely on me. Doesn't that make you feel better?"

Oddly enough, it didn't. Violet's heartfelt speech was wasted, and her imaginary Dante maintained a stony silence. In place of the grateful kisses she expected, all she got was an embarrassed shrug.

"But don't you understand, I love you."

Still no response.

"Aren't children impossible?" Violet sighed ruefully. "One gives and gives, but you can't make them take. At least I've tried my best."

Poor Violet was tired. The truly worst part of flying across the Atlantic was that it threw off your sleep schedule for days. It was not even nine o'clock and Violet was done in. She made a quick search of Dante's night table to see what kind of books he was reading. She found nothing of interest except the unfinished manuscript of *The Darkness of Daisy's Back Passage*. Violet took it to bed with her and fell asleep right after Mr. Camp was found dead.

Coming home later that night, Dante didn't notice his mother's dirty tea mug in the kitchen sink; nor was he alarmed by the smell of her cigarettes in the living room since Cecil had been smoking that afternoon; and while Audrey's room was right next to Violet's so that the sound of her snoring was unmistakable, Dante's bedroom was down the hall in the other direction. He woke up the next morning still blissfully unaware of his mother's presence.

Dante rolled over and rubbed his eyes. He had dreamt, just before waking, of having found the perfect ending for *The Darkness of Daisy's Back Passage*. What was it? Dreams being what they are, he couldn't remember, but the dream had given him hope and now he attacked the problem with renewed determination.

As you may recall, the beautiful Daisy murdered her rich husband for his money, and Caleb Astor, the handsome amateur sleuth, is in charge of bringing her to justice. Unfortunately, Daisy proves difficult to catch. She is too clever to be tricked into a confession (the game of *I Never*—Audrey nixed that) but what if, thought Dante staring up at his bedroom ceiling, she could be frightened into one?

With the morning light streaming in through his window, Dante imagined a dark and stormy night in the Hamptons. The wind howled, the shutters rattled, and the sky was inky black. The enterprising Caleb Astor had come up with a new plan. Long past midngiht, after all the other houseguests had fallen asleep, Caleb dressed himself in a long white sheet and snuck down the hall to Daisy's bedroom. The door creaked slightly as he opened it. Daisy tossed fitfully in her sleep. Caleb walked over to her, waved his arms slowly up and down, and spoke in a haunting voice:

```
                    CALEB
      Awake! I am the ghost of your dead
      husband come to exact retribution.
      You must confess your crime or I will
      follow you for the rest of your days.
      Repent! Confess!
```

Daisy was meant to wake up in a cold sweat. She was meant to see her husband's ghost (Caleb Astor in a white sheet), and get so scared that she'd confess to the murder. Caleb would tape record the confession, then dramatically pull off the sheet to reveal his true identity, and Daisy would break down in uncontrollable tears as the police sirens approached.

```
      Slow pan out across the Long Island Sound.
      The desperate loneliness of the water.
                    THE END!!!
```

That was how it was meant to work, but Daisy refused to cooperate. No matter how hard the wind blew, no matter how much the shutters rattled, Daisy simply wouldn't be fazed by the sight of Caleb in a white sheet.

```
                    CALEB
      Awake! I am the ghost of your dead
      husband come to exact retribution.
      You must confess your crime or I will
      follow you for the rest of your days.
      Repent! Confess!

                    DAISY
                  (angrily)
      What are you doing in my bedroom
      young man?
```

No good at all. Dante re-imagined the scene but this time Daisy got all sexy and purred like a kitten.

```
            DAISY
        (huskily)
What are you doing in my bedroom
young man?
```

That didn't work either.

Dante was about to try the scene again when he was startled out of his reverie by the sound of Audrey's voice saying good-bye to someone. Goodbye to whom? The front door closed, and moments later Dante heard footsteps approaching in the hallway. He froze in bed and tried to keep absolutely still, but the tension was too much for him. He crept out from under the sheets and went to listen at the door. It was his mother, he was sure, but perhaps if she thought he was asleep she would leave without waking him. Quiet as a mouse, Dante took another step towards the door. He thought he could hear someone breathing on the other side of it, and he waited, counting silently to himself. One thousand, two thousand, three thousand:

"Ow!"

The door opened suddenly with the corner of it catching Dante hard on the chin, and he fell backwards and landed heavily on the floor.

"What on Earth?" said Violet quizzically.

"Good morning, mother," said Dante.

"Get up, darling, and get dressed. I'm in the kitchen."

Dante did as he was told.

"You do sleep late," said Violet pouring Dante a cup of coffee. "I think you should make more of an effort. Early to bed early to rise."

Dante tasted the coffee, added two teaspoons of sugar, and for the first time in his life he wished he had a job to go to.

Six months ago, a week ago, last Friday for that matter—if Dante had been assigned an examination essay last Friday on the topic "Drawbacks Of Losing My Employment With Bullard & Associates" he would have run out of material before finishing a single sentence. But today he could have filled up three blue books without even pausing for breath, and as Violet rambled on, Dante outlined the benefits of office life in his head:

#1. You get your own desk.

#2. You can work on your screenplay in peace.

#3. YOUR MOTHER'S NOT THERE!

He put the last point in mental caps because it was by far the most important. The other benefits of office life all flowed from point #3 and were subsidiary to it. In fact, if you turned things around and your mother was at the office, then the list made no sense and you were better off at home.

"Dante!" said Violet, cutting herself off in mid-sentence. "You're not even listening."

"What were you saying?"

"I was saying that I love you and I've been blathering for ages. For heaven's sake, stop daydreaming. The least you could do is interrupt me."

"Sorry, I was thinking."

"About what?"

"Nothing, mother."

"Then pay attention. What's this Audrey tells me about going to Iowa? Why does she want to move to Iowa?"

"It has to do with her stipend. She wants a doctorate and she can get more money in Iowa than she can here."

"Surely you don't want her to leave."

"Of course not."

"Then tell her not to go. The stipend can't amount to much. I'd be willing to make up the difference if it means keeping her around."

"I've thought of that. Audrey wouldn't take it."

"Yes, you're probably right. I dropped a hint this morning and she became quite stroppy."

"I can't believe stroppy's the right word," said Dante, rising to Audrey's defense. "I've never seen her stroppy."

"Alright, but she did make a little speech about not wanting to live off other people's charity. It's quite childish in my opinion. Independence is all well and good, but a woman can't be picky about her sources of income."

"It doesn't help to criticize."

"I'm not criticizing, I just want her to see reason," Violet replied. "Now let's talk about your screenplay. I've made a few notes and I'd like to go through them with you."

"When did you read my screenplay?"

"Last night, darling. I finished it this morning."

"Shouldn't you have asked my permission first?"

"Don't be silly. You left it out in plain sight, and you know very well there's no point in writing something if no one else is allowed to read it. Besides, I thought it was quite good. The ending doesn't work but that's easily salvageable. It's nothing to be ashamed of. Do you think there's any chance of selling it?"

Dante brightened. He couldn't help but feel pleased by his mother's interest. "Cecil thinks there might be. He works for a big movie producer now."

"I heard. Max something, isn't it?"

"Max Guberstein," said Dante. "He's up for election at the Avenue and if he gets in, Cecil says he might buy the rights to my screenplay."

Violet smiled and looked thoughtful, "How is Cecil?"

"Fine, I guess. You can ask him yourself if you want. He's coming over after I get back from the club tonight. I'm supposed to tell him everything that happens at the admissions committee meeting."

"Why does Cecil care?"

"Because Max is his boss. If Max doesn't get elected, he's going to blame Cecil."

"That doesn't sound fair."

"No, but apparently it's how Max operates. If Max doesn't get into the club, he'll put Cecil on his blacklist and Cecil won't be able to work in the movies anymore. He'll have to return to London."

"But Penelope's in London," said Violet.

"The nail on the head, mother. Cecil would have to move back in with her and there'd be nothing to stop them getting married."

"Oh dear."

Dante shrugged. He sympathized with Cecil, but he didn't want his mother to get sidetracked. He needed Violet to stay focused, and whatever it was she'd come to do, he wanted her to do it quickly. Nothing should interfere with her boarding a plane back to Heathrow as soon as possible.

"Audrey said you have some business to take care of. What sort?" asked Dante.

"I've decided to let Puff buy the cottage in Long Island," Violet replied. "Gascon's opening a new restaurant and I promised to put up the money."

"Have you spoken to Puff yet?"

"I left him a message. It's only a matter of working out the details."

"Have you agreed on a price?"

"Not yet, but Puff wouldn't dare haggle with me."

"You're sure he wants to buy the cottage?"

"Puff has wanted to buy the cottage for donkey's ears. The whole thing can be settled in a day or two."

Dante let out a long breath and Violet looked at him sharply.

"Don't look so relieved, darling, you'll hurt your poor mother's feelings. Now what are we going to do today? I thought we might go to the museum, then have a nice lunch and a walk through the park."

9

After a long day with his mother, largely spent trying to convince her that he could take care of himself, Dante was relieved to be safe within the oak paneled confines of the Avenue Club. It was six o'clock and the admissions committee was gathered around a dining table in the Package Room.

The Package Room was a place of special significance to members of the Avenue Club. It got its name during Prohibition when the space was used as a liquor vault, and in the old days its only door was hidden behind a sliding bookcase in the library. A second door had since been added and the Package Room was now easily accessible, but it still served as a reminder of government's tendency to overreach.

At the head of the table, Dick Burkus took a sip of whiskey and tapped his wine glass with a fork. Standing up from his chair, he started in on a long joke about a man who mistakes a penguin for a nun. The other six members of the committee remained seated, listening patiently. On one side of the dining room, Dante was squeezed between John Newbury and Mr. Wainwright; on the other side, Mr. Bullard sat next to Ben Jentsen and Mr. Sears. Everyone waited for Dick to finish his joke.

"I tolla you," said Dick, the joke called for an Italian accent, "I tolla you, you fucka da penguin!"

Dick exploded with laughter, and Wainright and Sears snapped their fingers to signal their appreciation. Then Dick gulped down the rest of his whiskey and looked around the room:

"Everyone's here, let's get going. Can I have a motion?"

For reasons unknown, a great deal of life at the Avenue Club was governed by Robert's rules of parliamentary order. And not just the official meetings. You could hardly ask for a drink at the bar without someone demanding the request be motioned and seconded.

"I motion to begin the meeting," barked Wainwright.

"Second?"

"I second the motion," said Newbury. Newbury, whom Max referred to as Happy Boy, rarely voiced an opinion at the committee meetings but he liked seconding motions.

"Motion seconded," said Dick. "Let's eat."

One of the perks of being on the admissions committee was that you got a meal out of it, and the first course on tonight's menu was a country pâté. As the men started in, a matronly waitress in a black and white uniform went around the table pouring wine. Dick Burkus gulped his wine and chomped his food energetically. Little bits of goose liver fell out the sides of his mouth.

Wainwright turned to Dante and flashed him the hairy eyebrow. He really did look like a retired English Colonel.

"Welcome aboard, Dante. You've picked a good night to start. Veal chops. Can't go wrong with a veal chop."

Dante smiled politely. Having never been to a committee meeting before, he wondered when the actual work would begin. Dick Burkus had a stack of papers beside him but he was busy eating and he appeared in no rush to get to them.

Indeed, there was no rush.

The business of the evening was simply to discuss the candidates for admission, but since there were only five men up for election in the spring cycle, and since the committee had already been debating their various merits for almost two months, there was no reason not to enjoy dinner. No one expected any bombshells. Most of the committee's time would be taken up with small talk, and the remainder would be used to re-hash what was said about the candidates the week before.

The admissions committee worked at a leisurely pace, and although everyone acknowledged that the meetings were much longer and more numerous than was strictly necessary, there were also good reasons for proceeding slowly. For one thing, the candidates who didn't get into the club were more likely to take offense at decisions made in haste. And for another, it was understood that some of the most important personal information takes time to drip out.

To give an example: two years ago Dick Burkus put up for election a good friend of his named Conrad Steel. Six of the seven committee members were strongly in favor of Steele's admission, but the amiable John Newbury was, from the first instant, staunchly opposed. This was curious because

Newbury had never opposed a candidate before, and it was even more curious because he refused to give any reason for his opposition except to say that Steele rubbed him the wrong way. The committee's discussion went on for weeks without reaching a satisfactory consensus. Despite Steele's many supporters, Newbury consistently vowed to throw the blackball but he refused to say why. Finally Dick Burkus threw up his hands.

"Dammit, you're not being fair," he told Newbury. "You can't blackball a man who's a good friend to all of us without at least giving us a reason. If you want to stay on this committee you owe us an explanation. What have you got against the man?"

Newbury gritted his teeth and let it out: "Conrad Steele screwed my wife."

That sort of information was worth waiting for and it was exactly why the admissions committee proceeded as slowly as it did.

The waitress brought in the veal chops and Dick Burkus shuffled through his notes.

"First of all, I'd like to thank Dante Penfield for joining us. I know it's very last minute, but Dante's sitting in for Jos Nichols as the representative of our young membership and he'll be voting with us in the elections next week. Thanks for coming Dante." Dante nodded. "Now on to the candidates. The first name on the list is Charlie Blister. I don't think we need spend too much time on him."

Wainwright made a friendly growling sound and repeated verbatim what he'd said at the previous meeting:

"Danny Blister's son. Exeter, Dartmouth and Piping Rock.

He works at Morgan. I think you'd have to say he'll be an asset to the club. Good squash player, too."

All the heads around the table nodded.

"Anything to add, Dante?" asked Dick. Since it was his first meeting Dick wanted to make an effort to include him.

"No," said Dante hesitantly. The air of expectation in the room made him think he should say more, but he couldn't think what. Dante's circle of acquaintance was narrow. He knew Charlie Blister only slightly and he didn't care whether Blister joined the club or not but that wasn't an appropriate comment so he coughed into his hand while trying to think of a better one. At last Dante was ready to pronounce Danny Blister a very fine fellow indeed, but he didn't get the chance. Dick had moved on.

The committee worked through the first three candidates in a matter of minutes. The discussion went quickly because all three were assured of getting in. They were young men from good families who had gone to good schools, and they were well bred, friendly and most importantly, they were all under thirty years old.

Although it wasn't stated policy, an interesting thing about the Avenue Club was that it was much easier to join at the age of twenty-five than at the age of fifty-five. A blank sheet of paper arouses no passions. The secret to admission was not to have enemies and young men tend to have few of them. Older men had it much harder. Because if you've worked in New York for thirty years and you've had any sort of success it's almost certain there are people who hate you for it. And if any of those people happen to be members of the club, you're done for.

An illustration of this point could be seen in comparing the cases of Charlie Blister, a junior analyst at Morgan, and Derek Cairn, who sat on the bank's board of directors. Blister was twenty-six years old, had done nothing in his life, and would get into the club. Cairn was approaching sixty, was one of the most powerful men on Wall Street, and he had been blackballed the previous year on account of a decades old business dispute with Mr. Sears' brother-in-law.

Dick Burkus paused briefly before announcing the next name up for discussion.

"Darius Vajpayee." He allowed himself a smile. "Dot not teepee."

Darius' candidacy was noteworthy because Darius was an Indian. He was the eldest son of a wealthy Bombay industrialist and he had lived in New York since coming to the States as a university student. After graduation Darius had started a successful hedge fund and went on to marry a girl named Sally Thomas. Sally came from a distinguished New England family and her father, Hammy Thomas, was a long standing member of the Avenue Club.

"What I want to know," said Wainwright, "Is where did he prep?"

It was a rhetorical question, but to Wainwright, who clung sentimentally to his boarding school days, it was revealing. He believed that a man's prep school was the single most important influence on his character.

"Nobody knows," said Dick playing along. "Somewhere in India, I suppose."

"Right," said Wainwright taking a hard line, "And here's what I say. I had lunch with Mr. Vajpayee and I thought him a decent man. He wasn't forthcoming about his business dealings but I don't hold that against him. What I do hold against him is the high horse he's riding on. He says he's Indian aristocracy, son of a Rajah or something, but I say this club isn't the place for Rajahs. The Avenue is for ordinary people like you and me, and I don't want to come to the club worried about being on my best behavior because I might accidentally offend the Prince of Satrap."

Wainwright's argument was ingenious. His brain had inverted the facts to make it seem that he was the victim of Mr. Vajpayee's prejudice rather than the other way round. Wainwright continued:

"I'm leaning against it. I'm not saying definitively I'll blackball, but I'm leaning that way. It's a slippery slope and Mr. Vajpayee represents the tip of an iceberg. If he joins this year, then next year we'll be asking ourselves whether to elect Mr. Vajpayee's good friend Mr. Sinbad. Where did Sinbad prep? Somewhere in India most likely. Soon we'll turn ourselves into another United Nations like everything else. The Avenue wasn't meant for that. Our club has a special quality and we have an obligation to preserve it."

Dick munched on his chop.

Jentsen, who thus far had said nothing at the meeting, took his turn to speak. Jentsen was the man Max described as a bleeding heart:

"Let's not worry so much about where a man went to school. Mr. Vajpayee is an outstanding candidate. I had dinner with him a few weeks ago and I could not have been more impressed. He's well read, he's charming, and this isn't a question of slippery slopes. Mr. Vajpayee is one man, and a good man at that. He's just the sort of person I want to run into here."

Sears, a pragmatist, listened patiently then addressed a general question to the table.

"Shouldn't we be asking about Mr. Vajpayee's relationship with his father-in-law? How does Hammy Thomas feel about the candidacy?"

Sears had put his finger on it. This was the central question. Hammy Thomas was extremely well liked at the club and if Hammy pushed hard enough, Mr. Vajpayee could get past Wainwright's objections. But it was unclear how hard Hammy intended to push.

"I've heard the relationship isn't ideal," said Dick. "Of course, Hammy wrote a glowing letter of recommendation for Mr. Vajpayee, but as we all know these letters are sometimes written for public consumption. I've heard rumors that Hammy has had private discussions with members that cut the other way."

Jentsen was annoyed by Dick's knowing tone and his reference to whispered confidences: "Lots of rumors go around and lots of them aren't true. The committee shouldn't base its decisions on rumors."

Dick let the remark pass. It wasn't really a question of rumors, but he chose not to go into detail. Dick knew what he knew, and what he knew was this: Hammy Thomas had cornered him in the dressing room three weeks ago and told him point blank that he didn't want Mr. Vajpayee to get elected.

"You know I had to write that recommendation," Hammy said, "But I get plenty of Vajpayee on family holidays, I don't need him at the club, too."

The dinner plates were cleared and the matronly waitress brought out a Baked Alaska. Coffee and brandy were served.

Dick announced the last name on his list.

"Max Guberstein."

Dante had let his mind wander during the conversation about Mr. Vajpayee but now he woke up and paid close attention. Jentsen was the first to comment.

"President of GoldStream Pictures. Max Guberstein has come from humble beginnings and accomplished a great deal. I'm for him."

"Humble beginnings aren't all they're cracked up to be," said Wainwright. "He used to run a dry cleaners."

Dick had spilled some of the veal gravy on his shirt earlier in the evening. He pointed to the stain, "Do you think he could get this out?"

"No," Wainwright replied, "But I bet he'd charge you a lot for trying!"

Sears stepped in: "The dry cleaning business was a long time ago. Max is a businessman like the rest of us and he's a talented one. He's well connected and he knows people in city government. He could be very useful to the club. I'd be pleased to have Max as a member. He's a sharp man."

Everyone at the table was somewhat surprised by this endorsement. Sears was a blue blood of the first water, a snob to rival Wainwright, and in earlier meetings he had been very cool on Max. Now his tune had changed and the other members of the committee wondered why. Sears let them wonder. He felt no need to mention that his daughter had recently opened a bar in Soho and that Max had been instrumental in helping her get a liquor license. Wainwright picked up the thread.

"Too sharp by half if you ask me," he spluttered. "The club doesn't need sharp men. And frankly, I still don't understand why Mr. Guberstein is so eager to become a member. He's lived in New York all his life. If he was an Avenue man don't you think he would have tried to join the club twenty years ago? I suspect he's just looking for another feather in his cap. Is that what the club is for? How did he get so interested in the Avenue in the first place?"

"He's a friend of Puff's," said Dick. He looked to Mr. Bullard for confirmation. "Isn't that right?"

"Not just Puff," said Bullard. "Max has a lot of friends. Don't forget he's collected fourteen letters of recommendation from our fellow members and, to my knowledge, no one has written against him."

Dick wasn't satisfied. "How much does Puff care about this guy?"

"Puff is strongly behind him. Very strongly."

"Why?"

"I suppose you'd have to ask Puff," said Bullard. "But whatever his reasons, he is the club president and I think we owe his opinion a certain respect."

"Bullard has a point," said Wainwright, his opposition softening. "The president deserves a voice. What do you think, Dick?"

"I'm gonna reserve judgment. I've only met Max once and that was just a handshake. I'm having dinner with him on Friday, and I'll make my mind up then." It was late in the game for Dick to be having his first dinner with Max, but Dick often chose to wait until the last minute before meeting with a controversial candidate. It gave him more power because it meant the rest of the committee had less time to second guess his decisions. Dick nodded towards Dante. "How about you, Dante? Have you met Guberstein yet?"

"Only briefly."

"Then I want you to join me for my dinner with Max. We'll liquor him up and see what he's made of." Like the ancient Persians, Dick was a great believer in the revelatory power of alcohol. He tossed back his brandy. "You never really know a man until you've gotten drunk with him."

Dante remembered his run in with Max at Trixie's garden party. The prospect of a booze fest was unsettling: "What if Mr. Guberstein doesn't drink?"

"Doesn't drink!" exclaimed Wainwright.

"I don't know. Maybe he doesn't."

"That's bullshit," said Dick. "Hollywood bullshit."

"Don't be ridiculous," said Jentsen. "If a man chooses not to drink that's perfectly alright with me."

"Bullshit," said Dick again. "The only excuse for a teeto-taler is alcoholism, and as far as I know Guberstein's not an alcoholic, is he Bullard?"

"No, he's not," said Bullard.

"Right," said Dick. He turned to Jentsen. "Listen, the Avenue is many things but mostly it's a social club. Part of being

112

social is having a drink. Isn't that fair? I never want to see the day when I walk into the bar and find all the backgammon players sipping seltzer and Diet Coke. So I'm going to buy Guberstein a scotch, and if he's not gracious enough to drink it, then as far as I'm concerned he's not gracious enough to be a member of our club."

"Well put," said Wainwright.

Jentsen didn't care to argue the point and there was no further discussion of Max's candidacy. The meeting dissolved into a general debate about the economic benefits of cutting the capital gains tax. Finally, much as he had done at the start of the evening, Dick clanged dessert fork against his empty wine glass.

"Motion?" he said.

"Motion to end the meeting!" barked Wainwright.

"Second?"

"I second the motion," Jentsen replied.

"Thank you," said Dick. "Motion seconded. The meeting's over. I'll see everyone at the elections next Tuesday night."

10

The chirp of the cell phone next to Cecil's ear woke him up from a deep sleep. The night before, after a quick hour with Dante to talk over the admissions committee meeting, Cecil had gone out with Cat Penfield to a party hosted by one of her boarding school classmates. The party had given him nightmares and Cecil dreamt that he and Cat were married to each other. They were walking around Central Park together and every few paces they ran into a young man in a blazer who wanted to discuss the stock market. Still dreaming, Cecil now found himself on a ski slope. He was stuck in the snow and unable to move. Cat was there too, but somehow she had turned into Penelope, and she was laughing as Cecil struggled desperately to get up.

The cell phone rang again.

Cecil was hung-over. His head ached and his mouth felt as though he'd swallowed a cup of cake flour. He took a quick look around the hotel room and saw that he was alone. Enormously reassuring. He'd promised himself not to go to bed with Cat at least until after the club elections and so far he'd kept his promise. It was not yet seven o'clock in the morning. Cecil picked up the phone and heard a woman's voice.

"Good morning, darling. Can you hear me?"

"Of course I can. Hi."

"I do hope you're alright. Is Max keeping you busy?" It was Penelope calling from London.

"I've been running around like a dervish," said Cecil. He never spoke to Penelope without claiming to be inundated with work and he began telling her about Max, and the Avenue Club, and the need to make nice with Cat Penfield.

"Is she pretty darling?"

"Pretty enough."

"Then I'm sure you'll do fine." Penelope wanted to move on. "I don't have all day, dearest. I'm just calling before I go to yoga class. There's something we have to discuss."

"What is it?"

"It's Bruce."

Cecil could not remember a Bruce. Penelope continued:

"I'm sorry darling, but I'm very cross with you. I'm going to have to be quite firm."

"Who's Bruce?"

"The antique shop, darling." Of course, Bruce from the antique shop. Penelope was rabid for him. "I wrote a check last week, darling, and this morning I got a note from Bruce in the mail. Do you know what it said?"

"I don't."

"Well take a bloody guess, dear! It said insufficient funds! My check was returned to the shop because you never paid my overdraft!"

Cecil clasped his hand to his forehead, "I'm sorry."

"Of course you're sorry, but it's not very nice for me, is it? You promised you'd take care of the overdraft three weeks ago. Now Bruce wants to get paid and he is being quite difficult. He suggested I might have to return the gorgeous side table in my study. How do you think that makes me feel? It's awfully irresponsible of you, darling."

"I promise I'll take care of it as soon as possible."

"You know I'm alone here," said Penelope. There was a catch in her throat. "While you're busy flirting with pretty girls in New York, I'm struggling to keep the house up all by myself. The least you could do is keep track of the bank accounts. It's not right, darling."

Cecil's cell phone beeped.

"Hold on a second, I have another call."

"Cecil!" cried Penelope.

"Hello?" said Cecil.

"Meeting!" bellowed Max.

"Penelope?" said Cecil.

"Don't you dare hang up on me, darling. I'll be very cross!"

"I have to. It's Max." Cecil hung up on her. "Max?"

"Meeting!"

"I've just woken up."

"Extremely important meeting!"

Cecil's phoned beeped.

"I'm sorry Max, could you just hold for one moment. Hello?"

It was Penelope.

"I am very cross, darling!"

"I'll take care of it this afternoon. Tell Bruce he'll have his money tomorrow."

"But what about me, darling? I look like a ragamuffin. I need something to wear."

"Whatever you want, I have to go."

"Well don't forget. Kisses, darling. You do know I love you?"

"I love you too." Cecil switched back to the other line. "Max?"

Max had already hung up and the line was dead. Cecil dialed him back but there was no answer.

"Cat piss," said Cecil.

There was nothing to do but hurry to the Pierre Hotel.

Unshowered and unshaved, Cecil found Max in the hotel dining room. He was drinking herbal tea and making phone calls, and Cecil had to stand waiting in silence for a long while before Max deigned to speak to him.

"Never put me on hold again."

"Good morning, Max."

"Sit down, you shit."

Fortunately, this was a term of endearment, and it was the signal that Max's anger had passed. Cecil sat down.

"What did you want to see me about?"

"I'll run the meetings if you don't mind. You want some breakfast?"

"No, thanks."

"So, have you been enjoying yourself with Cat Penfield? How was the party last night?" Cecil hadn't told him about the party, but as always Max had done his homework. "Just remember to keep it in your pants until after the election. I don't need Mr. Penfield worried about his daughter's virtue."

"He's an odd man, Puff, isn't he?"

"Not what I'm used to," Max replied with surprising frankness.

"I met him at the bar after Cat's performance," Cecil went on. "He seemed very keen to find friends in common so I had to invent an uncle Peter to make him feel better. By the way, I lent him a photograph of yours. Mrs. Schuler gave it to me when I went to visit. She wanted you to have it, but Puff saw it at the bar and asked if he could hold on to it for a few days. It's a picture of your family under an awning on Fifth Avenue. You never told me you had a sister, Max."

"What sister?"

"I don't know, the girl in the picture. I assumed she was your sister."

"And you gave it to Penfield?"

"Well, it was taken outside Puff's apartment building and he wanted to make a copy. He probably has some historical interest in the architecture. There was no polite way to refuse."

"A refusal is never polite, you idiot. Doesn't mean you can't refuse."

Max closed his eyes and massaged his temples. He was an intensely private man and it should have been obvious to Cecil that he didn't want his family photos traded around.

"Are you alright, Max?"

"I have to make some calls."

Cecil shrugged.

"In private!" Max screamed. "Go wait on the street. I'll have someone fetch you when I'm ready."

Outside the Pierre, Cecil sat down on a fire hydrant and watched the dog walkers heading off to Central Park. He could never predict Max's temper and he wondered what had provoked it. Possibly the photograph, but who knows? Working for Max was hellish. Cecil smoked a cigarette. He crossed his fingers and dreamed about how much better life would be if he got the new job at SouthEnd Pictures.

Twenty minutes later a waiter popped his head outside the hotel and told Cecil he could go back in.

"What was that about?" asked Cecil.

"Let's move on," Max replied. "I assume you've spoken to your friend by now."

"Dante? Yes, I have."

"I want to know what happened at the committee meeting. Where did Mr. Bullard come down?"

"Strongly in support. He said Puff very much wants you in."

"Hmpphh," grumbled Max, "Let's hope it sticks. Go on."

Cecil took out a small note pad and flipped through it.

"Alright, here's the run down. Newbury didn't say anything but apparently he never does."

"He's an imbecile," said Max.

"Then you've got Jentsen, the bleeding heart. He's on your side and says he admires what you've accomplished in life given your humble beginnings."

Max winced.

"You've also got Mr. Sears lined up. Sears said he thinks your connections in city government will be useful to the club. He called you a sharp man."

"As a compliment?" asked Max.

"Dante thought so." Cecil suppressed a smile.

Max did not like Sears calling him sharp. It was a code word. To men like Sears, a sharp man meant a sharp dealer, which always meant a Shylock. It was a backhanded reference to Jewishness, and although Max knew he was sharp and he knew he was Jewish, it infuriated him when dull minds linked the two traits together.

"What about Wainwright?" asked Max.

"Outspokenly negative. He doesn't want sharp men in the club and doesn't think you're Avenue material."

"Asshole."

"But you still need his vote."

"Wainwright's a jellyfish," Max snorted. "He swims with the tide. He'll come along if I get the rest of them. The real concern is Dick Burkus. What did he say?"

"Non-committal. He said he's reserving judgment on your candidacy until he gets to know you better."

"I'm having dinner with him Friday night."

"Presumably what he was referring to. Actually you're having dinner with two people. Dick asked Dante to come with him. They discussed it at the meeting."

"Shouldn't make a difference."

"No," said Cecil, "But you're not going to like what comes next."

Max raised an eyebrow.

"Dick is planning to get you drunk."

"But I don't drink," said Max.

"You may have to. Dick seems to think that drinking is an admissions requirement."

"Impossible. I haven't had a drink since I was nineteen years old. Alcohol gives me a rash."

"Dick said that if you're not gracious enough to drink with

him then you're not gracious enough to join the Avenue. I don't see any way around it."

Max was annoyed but he understood that Dick Burkus held all the cards.

"It's not going to help if I vomit on the tablecloth."

"I wouldn't suggest it," said Cecil. "But there are alternative solutions. My aunt, Lady Foster, was once asked to entertain a group of Soviet diplomats at her home in Somerset. The secret service wanted her to get the Soviets drunk to see if they'd give anything away. The trouble, of course, was that Lady Foster would have to get drunk too and she was a very small woman. Three glasses of vodka and she'd pass out before the Russians even felt tipsy."

"The point is?"

"The point is that the secret service told her to eat half a pound of butter half an hour before her guests showed up. She tried it, and she drank everyone under the table without feeling a thing. She woke up the next morning fresh as a daisy."

"Is that a fucking joke?" asked Max.

"No, it's absolutely true."

"Then you can shove it up your ass. I'm not eating half a pound of butter."

"I didn't think you would," said Cecil. "But I've given the matter some thought and I do have one other idea."

"What is it?"

Cecil told him.

"It better work," said Max.

11

"I could never wear that," said Rebecca Holland, glancing over the fashion pictures in the *Style* section of the Thursday morning paper. She reached for the sugar bowl and added a half teaspoon to her coffee. The teaspoon was engraved, in the confusing way of silver monograms, with the initials DBE. The *E* stood for Edwin.

Rebecca still paid rent on a small apartment in Chelsea, but she spent most of her nights, and kept most of her clothes, at Dick's place on 83rd and Park.

"Sure you don't want a ride with me?" asked Dick. He was dressed in docksiders, khaki shorts and a pink polo shirt. Like Rebecca he was on his way out to Long Island. He had to get his boat back in the water in time for the opening of Yacht Club. "Seems silly to take two cars. You could drop me off at the house and pick me up after you talk to Draper."

"I need my own car," said Rebecca. "Who knows how long you'll be and I have to be back in the city at two o'clock. I'm having lunch with Alice Theobold."

"You really think you'll get something out of her?"

"I might."

"Well, good luck." Dick kissed Rebecca on the forehead. "I'm off to the country without you."

Rebecca smiled. It amused her that Dick always referred to Long Island as "the country." As if the north shore were a rural wilderness populated by farmers and lumberjacks.

She drank her coffee and finished reading the paper. Rebecca had a busy day ahead. First she had to drive out to Oyster Bay to meet Andrew Draper; then she had to rush back to Manhattan in time for a late lunch with Alice Theobold; and she would have to stay on her toes the whole time.

Both of Rebecca's meetings that day had a single purpose, and it was investigative rather than social. For the last month, she had been quietly working on a magazine article about the naughty, tell-all novel *Paisley Mischief.* She envisioned it as a high society piece, a literary whodunit full of gossip and betrayed friendship, and she had already sold the pitch, but in order to get into print she had to solve the central mystery of her story: she had to name the novel's anonymous author. Naming the author was the key, and although Rebecca had a pretty good idea who it was, she wasn't yet certain. Hence the meetings with Draper and Alice. Andrew Draper was the retired insurance salesman who collected antiques, rented a cottage from Dolly Smith, and was widely rumored to have written *Paisley Mischief.* Alice Theobold was the fountainhead itself. She was the novel's publisher.

Rebecca took out her copy of *Paisley Mischief* and leafed through it once again. She had read it many times over but she

wanted to refresh her memory, and she paid special attention
to the dialogue because she wanted a sense of the author's
voice. She noted, among other things, that the characters
cursed both frequently and expressively, and she wondered
whether Mr. Draper would curse like that in person. An hour
later she was at his doorstep ready to find out.

"Hello. You must be Rebecca."

Andrew Draper sounded faintly girlish and he stood in
the doorway wearing baggy blue swim shorts under a white
oxford shirt. He was tall and fat and he looked about sixty
years old. He was holding a silver porringer in his hand.

"Isn't that pretty," said Rebecca. "What is it, an ashtray?"

"It's a porringer, for eating porridge. That's the English
word for oatmeal. Porringers used to be given to babies as
christening presents. This one was made in the 1860's."

"It's beautiful."

"Oh, I have much nicer ones inside. Come in, I'll show
you around."

Knowing that Mr. Draper not only collected, but also occasionally sold antiques, Rebecca had arranged her visit on
the pretext that she was interested in buying something. She
had telephoned a few days before, introducing herself as a
friend of Dolly's, and saying she needed something unique
for Dick's birthday.

"So you're looking for a present for your boyfriend," said
Mr. Draper cheerfully. "I suggest we start with a tour. I'll
show you what I've been collecting, and if anything strikes
your fancy, speak up. If I can't sell it to you myself, I'll tell you
where you can find something similar. Okay?"

You wouldn't think it would take long to tour a cottage, but Mr. Draper was an enthusiastic talker, and though there were only four rooms, each one was so overstuffed with knick-knacks and curios (*objets* as Mr. Draper called them) that it took ages to go through them. Despite having settled on a ceramic Japanese phallus early on, Rebecca could do nothing to cut it short, and after more than an hour, she was wilting. She still hadn't found an opening to discuss *Paisley Mischief*.

"Here's a good example of intaglio carving," Mr. Draper went on, "Intaglio is the opposite of cameo and has a negative image. This one's a copy from the Roman, but even the copies are quite rare."

"I need something to drink," said Rebecca.

"Would you like a cup of tea?"

Rebecca said she would and Mr. Draper led her to the kitchen. It was now or never and Rebecca took the bull by the horns. Pretending to rummage through her bag for a lip balm, she pulled out a copy of *Paisley Mischief* and banged it down on the kitchen table with an ostentatious thud. But Mr. Draper was busy with the kettle and didn't seem to notice. So Rebecca had to pick the book up and wave it in front of his face.

"What's that?" he asked.

"*Paisley Mischief.* Haven't you read it?"

"Sorry," said Mr. Draper. "I don't read much. I suppose I should but I don't. I watch television."

"You've never even heard of it?"

"Should I have? What's it about?"

"It's a novel," said Rebecca. "With a lot of gossip about

Dolly Smith's friends. It's got people very upset. Dolly hasn't mentioned it to you?"

"Dolly and I talk about antiques. We don't gossip about her friends."

"Not even a word about the book?"

"No."

"I'm surprised."

"Why?"

"Because," said Rebecca, "Whoever wrote *Paisley Mischief* wrote it anonymously. And there's a rumor flying around that you're the author."

"Oh!" said Mr. Draper. He didn't swear, he just clapped his hand over his mouth and blushed. He looked quite as shocked as if he'd been caught with his pants down in church. "Why would anyone think I wrote that book?"

Rebecca explained that the author's pen name was Anne Smith. His name was Andrew and he rented from Dolly Smith. Andrew plus Smith, Anne Smith. That's how the rumor got started.

"But that's ridiculous!" said Mr. Draper. "Does Dolly know about this?"

"I'm sure she's heard the rumors."

"Then I'll speak to her at once. Thanks for telling me. I don't want her to think I've been doing anything behind her back."

Driving back to the city Rebecca took a series of mental notes. It was obvious to her that Andrew Draper had nothing to do with *Paisley Mischief*, but she would use her visit with him in the article anyway. Every good whodunit needs a red herring and Rebecca could get at least five hundred words out of the nice man who stuffed his cottage with antiques.

Old Money

The rough draft of a paragraph formed in her head:

> Wagging tongues at first suggested it was Andrew Draper
> who wrote the book everyone is talking about, but when I
> went out to interview him at his home, it was clear that Mr.
> Draper is not a novelist. He prefers watching television to
> reading, but his only real interest is antiques. He answered
> his doorbell holding a 19th century porringer in his hand.

Definitely include the porringer, thought Rebecca. She
considered how much to make fun of Mr. Draper's effeminacy.
Not too much because that would be unfair—besides it wasn't
the tone she was aiming for—but there was nothing wrong
with putting in one or two details nodding in that direction:

> Mr. Draper is an old bachelor with a soft, round face and a
> high-pitched voice. When I told him that he was rumored
> to be the author of Paisley Mischief, he clapped his hands
> over his mouth and squealed "Oh!" He could not have
> been more surprised if I'd asked him to marry me.

It was a good morning's work. Rebecca had never put any
faith in the Andrew Draper theory and she was pleased, not
only to be proven right, but also because Mr. Draper wasn't
charismatic enough to be the star of her article. She still didn't
know for sure who wrote *Paisley Mischief* but now there was
only one name left on her list of suspects, and if she got it
right, she'd have a very interesting story to tell indeed. All that
was left was to convince Alice Theobold to provide the confirmation, and as Rebecca drove back through the Midtown
Tunnel she felt a flutter of excitement rising in her tummy.

Lunch with Alice Theobold was at a quiet restaurant on West 11th Street, two blocks past Hudson. Alice had chosen the place because it was out of the way and she didn't want her meeting with Rebecca to be talked about by anyone in the office.

As the publisher of *Paisley Mischief*, Alice had pledged to keep the identity of its author a secret, and thus far she had kept her pledge. She was the only person in New York who knew where the royalty checks were sent. But Alice was too good a businesswoman to keep such a secret forever. She knew that a big feature in one of the weeklies would be invaluable publicity, and Alice believed that her duty to sell books trumped all other obligations. Of course she couldn't name names directly, but by agreeing to have lunch it was understood she was willing to be helpful. If Rebecca was looking in the right direction, Alice wasn't going to throw sand in her eyes.

"I love your jacket. Have you lost weight?"

"Thanks," said Alice smiling. "But no I haven't. I hope I didn't keep you waiting too long. You look great."

Rebecca ordered a bottle of white bordeaux and the conversation started off casually, with talk of mutual friends in the publishing business. Alice told a long story about a recently completed merger that had left her old boss without a job.

"Nowadays it's all money, money, money," she concluded mournfully, "Nobody cares about literature anymore, everyone talks about product. Sometimes I think I should have left New York years ago. Who needs it? I want to go to Vermont and live in the woods."

"You'd be hanging from the rafters within a week."

"I probably would," said Alice, "But it's a nice idea. What's new with you?"

"Working as usual."

"You said you wanted to talk to me about one of the books on my list."

"That's right," said Rebecca. "I'm doing research for a piece about *Paisley Mischief.* I'm sure you remember it. It's sort of a roman à clef and it's ruffled some feathers among the Park Avenue crowd."

Alice raised an eyebrow feigning surprise. "Are you part of that set?"

"A friend of mine is, so I see it second hand."

"What did you think of the book?"

"I liked it. But more than that, I think it's very good material for an article. People are talking and a lot of them are quite upset."

"Well, it is very racy in parts."

"It's not that," said Rebecca, knowing full well Alice didn't think it was. "The book appears to be based on real characters and real events, and that's what's got everyone riled up. They feel exposed."

"So you want to write about the truth behind the fiction. Is that it?"

"Yes and no," Rebecca replied. "I'll have to do some of that, but I'm more interested in how people have reacted to the book. I want to write about the storm in society's teacup, but in order to do that I have to find out who created the storm. The main thing is to figure out who wrote it. That's the important angle because that's what everyone wants to know."

"Do you have any ideas?"

"I do, I have a very good idea and I've got multiple sources on it. In fact, I could probably start writing tomorrow, but you know how it is, a journalist can never be too sure of herself. That's why I wanted to talk to you. I suppose you know who the author is?"

"I can't tell you."

"But you know?"

"Yes."

"Good. I'm not asking you to do my research for me, I just need confirmation. You won't have to say a word and if I'm wrong, I'll never ask you again. Okay?"

Alice remained silent as Rebecca picked up a cocktail napkin and continued, speaking quietly.

"I'm going to write the author's name down on this napkin and then I'm going to hand it to you. If I'm correct, put the napkin in your purse, otherwise give it back to me. Does that sound fair?"

Alice paused. She had promised not to reveal the author's identity, but if Rebecca had already figured it out on her own, it was giving nothing away to confirm her suspicions. Alice nodded her head ever so slightly and Rebecca wrote down a name on her napkin:

PENFIELD

Rebecca held her breath. Despite the show of confidence, it was really just a hunch, but it was a good hunch. Trixie Penfield had more friends than anyone so she was well placed to know the stories that made up *Paisley Mischief*. She was also smart and energetic and she had once been a lawyer so it was no stretch to imagine her writing a novel. Another telling point was that one of the novel's central figures was married to a character named Reggie "Stuffy" Canbrook. Canbrook bore a striking resemblance to Puff and there were details in the book about Puff's family history that only someone very close to him would know. Finally, there was the odd fact that Trixie herself was the source of so many rumors about the book's authorship. It was Trixie who started the rumor about Andrew Draper having written the book. And again it was Trixie who had pointed the finger at Rebecca as the possible author. Why would Trixie make such a fuss if not to draw attention away from herself?

Rebecca waited on the edge of her seat as Alice read the name on the napkin. Then calmly, wordlessly, Alice opened her purse and dropped the napkin inside.

Rebecca had her girl.

12

It was noon on Friday, and Puff sat in his study on the third floor of his 76th Street brownstone as the zee-zee-zee song of a newly arrived warbler drifted in through the window. Puff reached for the binoculars on his desk and went to the window to look for the warbler, but it was too well hidden to find. Zee-zee-zee, Puff hummed to himself. No small disappointment could dampen his mood. He had just finished negotiating with Violet for the purchase of her cottage on Long Island and they had shaken hands on the deal only ten minutes ago. Puff was inordinately pleased. He had always wanted the cottage and it would be perfect for Cat now that she was old enough to have a place of her own. All that was left was to draw up the papers and sign them.

Puff sat back down at his desk and hesitated for a moment trying to decide whether to call Cat, his banker, or his lawyer first, but before he could make up his mind, the telephone rang.

"Hello? Hello? Can I speak to Trixie?"

"Trixie's not in," said Puff. "Can I take a message?"

"Yes, you can Puff. It's Dolly here, Dolly Smith. I have some important news and I think you need to hear it, too. Are you familiar with a novel called *Paisley Mischief*?"

Puff furrowed his brow. "I'm familiar with it. I haven't read it."

"Tasteless drivel."

"I'd rather not discuss it."

"I feel exactly the same way," said Dolly. In the heat of the moment she forgot the countless hours she'd spent talking about *Paisley Mischief* with her girlfriends. "But I'm afraid we have to discuss it now. I had a visit this morning from my tenant, Mr. Draper. Do you know him?"

"I don't."

"Well he's a very nice man and he was quite put out. He told me he'd seen Rebecca Holland yesterday, Dick's girlfriend, and she had the nerve to suggest that I'm the source for all the dirty gossip in the *Paisley* novel."

"I take it you're not."

"Certainly I'm not! That's not the point. The point is, Rebecca's a journalist and she was trying to find out if Mr. Draper was the anonymous author. Put two and two together, Puff. If you ask me, Rebecca's planning to write an article about the book. She didn't announce it in so many words, but it's the only explanation I can think of. Why else would she be poking around?"

"This isn't good," said Puff.

"No, it's awful. Can you imagine the publicity? I don't want photographers staked out on my front lawn."

Dolly was actually quite pleased at the thought of photographers staked out on her front lawn, but Puff took her at her word and he was thoroughly shaken. Despite that he had not read *Paisley Mischief*, and despite that he tried hard never to think about it, Puff was nonetheless aware that the novel made him an object of ridicule, and it was unimaginable to him that Dick would allow his girlfriend to write a magazine article drawing attention to the book.

"There won't be any photographers," said Puff determinedly. "There won't be any article either. Thank you for calling, Dolly."

Puff hung up and dialed Dick's cell phone but there was no answer. "He's at the club," Puff thought, which made sense because cell phone use was prohibited at the club. Puff put on his jacket, straightened his tie and steamed out of the house to hail a cab.

"The Avenue Club!" he barked at the driver.

The lunch hour was the busiest time of day at the Avenue. Many of the members worked in midtown and some of them ate lunch at the club five days a week. The younger members liked to play a quick game of squash and eat a niçoise salad; the older men preferred ten minutes on the stationary bike and creamed chicken (the creamed chicken was first rate); but for young and old alike, the Avenue was viewed as a midday refuge, an island of restfulness amid the screaming hullabaloo, and it was one of the club's oldest traditions that when a member entered, he was expected to leave his anger and frustrations at the door.

Puff had never broken with tradition before, but today he was on fire, and he allowed his anger to walk right into the club alongside him. Puff and his anger marched up to the front desk together, matching each other stride for stride, and it was such a startling breach of convention that Freddie was struck dumb for a moment. He forgot to say hello.

"Where's Dick Burkus?" Puff demanded. "Where is he?"

"I'm not sure, sir."

"Is he here? Is he in the club?"

"Yes, sir."

"Where?"

"I don't know."

Puff clapped his hands and climbed the stairs. On the second floor landing, he ran into a small crowd of members milling around outside the dining room.

"Puff!"

"Hello Puff."

"Good to see you Puff."

They all greeted him at once, but Puff was so intent on finding Dick that he didn't even acknowledge them, and this behavior was so unusual that the buzz spread quickly.

Puff looked everywhere. Dick wasn't in the bar and he wasn't in the library, he wasn't in the changing lounge or the swimming pool, and when Puff poked his head into the exercise room, all he saw was Mr. Bullard cheerfully sweating away on a rowing machine.

"Bullard!" said Puff.

"Must keep old bodies active," called Mr. Bullard, failing to catch Puff's tone. "You know what Jefferson said: a long walk will do more for a man's happiness than the deepest philosophy."

"Damn Jefferson. Where's Dick Burkus?"

Mr. Bullard didn't know and Puff pushed on. He climbed high into the nether regions—the squash courts, the racquets courts, the court tennis courts—but all without success, and by the time Puff returned to the busy changing lounge, his mood had translated itself into a general anxiety felt by everyone in the club. Finally, a young Haitian laundry boy brought the crisis to a head:

"Mr. Penfield, sir, I believe Mr. Burkus is in the smoking room."

"Bah!" said Puff.

The smoking room was the quiet hideaway tucked behind the walk-in humidor into which, for legal reasons, no employee was allowed to enter. It was filled with books, worn leather chairs, and enormous crystal ashtrays which the members emptied themselves, and because it was so closed off, the nervous tension that infected the rest of the building had not yet penetrated its walls. While Puff was raging, Dick Burkus had been sitting calm as a monk, sucking on one of his favorite cigars, and idly pondering the evening's dinner with Max.

"Dick!" said Puff.

"What brings you into this den of vice?" he replied.

It was a friendly enough question, but to Puff it was infuriating. There was Dick sitting deep in the bowels of the Avenue Club, enjoying every privilege of his class, while at the same time he was in cahoots with a tawdry journalist who intended to hold them all up for ridicule. It was outrageous and Puff flushed crimson.

"Hold on," said Dick. "If this is about the admissions

committee, don't waste your breath. I'm seeing Max tonight and I'll make up my own mind. I don't need your input and I don't want it."

"Hush! This is not about the admissions committee. This is about your nasty little girlfriend, Rebecca Holland."

"You better cool down old man," said Dick choosing not to take too much offense.

"I will not cool down. I have just learned that Rebecca is planning to write an article about *Paisley Mischief*."

"And so what if she is?"

"I won't stand for it, that's what! I refuse to let your girlfriend publicize that disgraceful book in the glossy pages of a cheap magazine. I'll have you kicked out of the club."

"Stop being an ass," said Dick, and to Puff's consternation, he actually smiled. "First of all, you know you could never kick me out of the club, and second of all, you're barking up the wrong tree."

"Rebecca's not writing an article?"

"Oh sure, there's an article, but you're angry at the wrong woman. You shouldn't be mad at Rebecca, she's doing you a favor."

"And how is that?"

"Better to lance the wound than let it fester," said Dick. "I assume you know that *Paisley Mischief* was written anonymously. Don't you know who wrote it?"

"Of course not."

"Well maybe you don't, but Rebecca does, and she got the name straight from the publisher. She told me about it in confidence last night, and the only reason she hasn't told anyone else yet is out of respect for your feelings." Dick took a drag on his cigar. "So leave Rebecca out of this. People in glass houses can't throw stones."

"I don't know what you mean."

"Really? You really want to tell me you don't know who wrote that book?"

"No!"

"Then I'm sorry for you, Puff. The author's name is Penfield. It's your wife."

Up until this last moment Dick had been enjoying the skirmish, but now Puff looked so stricken, and the pain on his face was so great, that there was no pleasure in witnessing it. Dick felt a surge of pity in his heart as Puff turned suddenly pale and left the smoking room.

"But for chrissake what an idiot," thought Dick, and soon his mind was back on Max Guberstein and the entertaining prospect of getting him drunk that night.

Dick's dinner with Max was set for seven, but at five thirty Cecil was already busy making arrangements with two waiters at a small French bistro on Horatio Street. Given the task of choosing the restaurant, Cecil picked Le Petit Chien for three reasons. Because French was always the safest bet, because Cecil himself ate there regularly and he trusted the staff, and finally because he figured that Dick had never been there before and likely would never go back.

Cecil spent a long while in planning and he didn't leave the restaurant until shortly before Dante showed up. Dante arrived typically early, but not wanting to be the first to sit down, he strolled over to the river and up through the meat packing district to pass the time. When he got back, Max and Dick were already at their table in the corner of the small, dark dining room. Max sat with his back to the wall and Dante noticed a beautiful, tall brunette at a table nearby. She looked bored drinking champagne by herself, probably waiting for her date.

"Come, come, Dante," said Max cheerfully. His manner was entirely different than it had been at Trixie's garden party.

"You're late!" cried Dick affably.

The geniality was only to be expected given the circumstances, but there was a false note in it that made Dante nervous. He felt as though he were interrupting the start of a chess match, and he found it difficult to act naturally because there were too many unanswered questions beneath the surface. Did Dick really have an open mind about Max, or was he simply out for blood? Could Max maintain his bonhomie throughout an entire meal? And how would Max avoid getting drunk? Taking a seat, Dante saw that his best course of action would be to keep out of the way as much as possible.

"I need a drink," said Dick, beckoning to a waiter. "What are you having Max?"

"Scotch on the rocks."

"I'll go along with that. You too, Dante. Let's make it three scotch on the rocks."

Dick spread his hands out on the starched white tablecloth and took a deep cleansing breath.

"Alright Max, I'm gonna put my cards on the table. I've heard a lot about you, and not all of it good, but I don't pay much attention to what other people say. There's a lot of pissants in the world. I've always made up my own mind and that's what I intend to do tonight. So let's just enjoy ourselves and see what happens. Agreed?"

"Agreed," said Max.

"So tell me, how'd you get interested in the Avenue Club? Did Puff put you up to it?"

"More or less."

"That's not a straight answer," said Dick. "I guess what I'm asking is, what's your relationship with Puff? I mean, what do you think of him personally?"

"What do I think of him, personally?" Max repeated the question in order to give himself time to think. It was early in the evening but he sensed a trap being laid.

"Do you think he's a good guy?" asked Dick. "Because, I'll be honest with you, I don't. I've known Puff all my life and I think he's a pain in the neck. If the stick was any further up his ass, he'd be a scarecrow."

Dick laughed loudly for a moment, then stopped suddenly and stared hard at Max waiting for a reaction. It was an aggressive line and it appeared to be a test of sorts. Max answered with conviction.

"Wallace Penfield is a good man and if you want to talk crap about him, I'm leaving. I'm not going to listen to it."

There was a short silence. Dante expected a blustery counter from Dick but none came. Instead he was gravely nodding his head.

"I like that, Max. The first rule of the Avenue is you have to stick up for your friends. That's good. I was giving you a chance to knife Puff in the back and you turned it down. I admire that."

Max glared at Dick. "If I think you're an asshole, I'll say it to your face."

"As it should be."

The waiter returned with the drinks. Dick took his scotch and raised it in salute. He and Max clinked glasses, and Dick threw his head back and guzzled. Dante kept his eyes on Max, who was swirling the ice cubes around in his glass. Was he going to drink it? Max put the scotch to his lips and swallowed a large swig. Then he snorted and let out a loud *aahh*.

"Hair on your chest," said Dick.

"Hair on your chest," echoed Max.

It looked like a scene from an old Western, rival gunslingers resolving their differences over a bottle of whiskey. Dick and Max continued drinking scotch after scotch all through dinner, and the more they drank, the more a giddy sort of camaraderie blossomed between them.

It turned out that Dick and Max had a good deal in common. They were both abrasive men and their shared contempt for the niceties of social discourse bound them together. They talked about money and film and politics, and as they were finishing their steaks, the talk turned to women.

"I hear you get incredible girls in the movie business."

"I guess. You can if you look for it. I'm getting too old for that now."

"Everyone slows down," said Dick sympathetically.

Just then the tall brunette who'd been drinking champagne by herself approached the table. The boyfriend had never shown up.

"Max Guberstein?" Her accent was faintly German. "I am Natasha. We met last week."

Natasha bent over to kiss Max's cheek and as she did so the front of her dress opened giving Dick an unobstructed view of her small, but marvelously firm and naked breasts.

"I remember you," said Max. "Natasha, this is my friend Dick Burkus."

"I am happy to meet you." Natasha smiled and kissed Dick on the cheek, letting her dress fall open again. She really did have glorious breasts. She turned back to Max. "I just wanted to say hello. "

"Thanks for stopping by." He patted Natasha on the ass and told her to have a good night. Then Max looked at Dante, addressing him directly for the first time all evening.

"What do you think of that?"

"Who is she?"

"She's a lingerie model, part of a special I'm putting together for AMC. You like her?"

"She's amazing."

Max grinned and wagged his finger. "I have to correct you there. Natasha's amazing, but the most amazing thing about her is that she's not a she. Her real name is Paul Wojscicki and the accent's an act. She's just a tough kid from Greenpoint."

Dante was non-plussed and he turned quickly in his seat to catch Natasha shimmying out of the restaurant. "She's a boy?"

Max winked at Dick and waited a beat to give him time to catch the joke. "If you believe that, young man, you're drunker than I thought. Where's a Brooklyn boy gonna get tits like that?"

"She's not a boy?" Dante was thoroughly confused.

"You need to get out more. Natasha is woman to the bone, and one of the sweetest, most docile girls you'll ever want to meet."

Dick burst out laughing. Played on Dante, it was a good trick and Dick was still laughing when the waiter came to clear the dinner plates.

"I had you all wrong, Max."

"Hey," replied Max modestly.

"No," said Dick. He was well drunk and he pressed his point. "No Max, I mean it. I had you all wrong. I don't want to mince words. I didn't expect to like you." He reached across the table and placed his hand on Max's forearm. Max fought back the desire the flinch. "We're from different worlds, Max. But it doesn't matter, does it? We're all the same in the end. Men are simple creatures. God put us on Earth to eat, drink and screw, and everything else is just bullshit. I don't care where you're from, Max. I've been called a lot of names in my time, but I've never been called a bigot. I judge people by who they are and how they act. Look at me, Max."

It was all Max could do not to slap him in the face.

"Look at me," Dick repeated. "You're okay, Max. You're okay with me. C'mon let's finish this round and have one last drink. You too, Dante."

The three men banged their rocks glasses together and drained them simultaneously. It was the fourth scotch of the evening, and for Dante it was one too many. He felt woozy and he was suddenly very thirsty. What he wanted was water, but the waiter brought whiskey so whiskey would have to do.

Dante snatched a glass off the tray before the waiter could hand it to him.

"Excuse me," said the waiter, "That's Mr. Guberstein's drink."

"It's all the same," said Dante. He took a sip and sighed with relief. "Oh, that's nice, much nicer than the last round. That's delicious."

"Give me that!" shouted Max.

"No wait," said Dick. "Give it to me."

Max and Dick both grabbed for the glass at the same time, and without thinking, Dante gave it to Dick.

Dick leaned back and shook his head, looking amused. "You're a devil, Max," he said teasingly. "You serve your guests a decent single malt, but I bet there's a bottle of Johnny Walker Blue in the back with your name on it. How's it feel to get caught? Not that I haven't done the same myself when I'm paying the bill." Dick sniffed his drink and took a long taste. An expression of extreme puzzlement registered on his face and he tasted it again.

"Fuck me, Max. This is apple juice."

Max remained silent.

He had never any intention of getting into a drinking contest with Dick Burkus, and on Cecil's advice he'd made a special arrangement with the restaurant. When Dick ordered scotch he would be served scotch; when Max ordered scotch he would be served a cold glass of apple juice.

"Apple juice!" cried Dick. "You've been drinking apple juice all night!" He could hardly believe it, and he searched Max's face for signs of drunkenness, but there weren't any. "You cunning bastard, you're sober as a judge!"

Old Money

Dick had never been so insulted in all his life and his new found affection for Max died on the spot. He stood up from the table, threw his napkin down with a flourish, and made one final remark before marching out:

"It'll be a cold day in hell, Max Guberstein, when you get elected to the Avenue Club."

13

Dante returned home from the restaurant to find Cecil, Audrey and his mother gathered in the living room waiting for his report.

"How'd it go?" asked Cecil.

"Not good."

"Not well," Violet corrected him.

"A total disaster."

Dante poured himself a large glass of water and told them the whole story of the dinner from start to finish. Just as he got to the end, and Dick's cold-day-in-hell remark, Cecil's cell phone rang.

"Max, I expect."

Cecil put the phone on speaker and laid it on the coffee table. A river of obscenities flowed out of the receiver. Max was so loud that the tinny sound of his ravings filled the entire room, and after listening in silence for a few minutes, Cecil shrugged and hung up on Max in mid rant.

"So?" asked Audrey.

"So, nothing." Cecil poured himself another sherry. He felt exhausted. "Fired and blacklisted, not even the secretaries will take my calls. There's no chance of getting the job with SouthEnd Pictures and my work visa expires in two months. It's back to London, I suppose."

"You mustn't go back," said Violet. "You'd have to move in with Penelope again, you'd have to marry her."

The mention of Penelope's name reminded Cecil that, on top of his other difficulties, he'd forgotten to put any money in her bank account. He put his head in his hands and sighed dramatically.

"Oh please," said Audrey. "Stop moaning."

"What else can I do?" he replied peevishly. "I can't stay in the States without a job and I can't get a job if Max doesn't want me to."

"Why didn't you tell me Max was drinking apple juice?" said Dante.

"It's not your fault," Cecil reassured him.

"Quite right it's not his fault," said Audrey.

Violet spoke more encouragingly. "There must be something you can do. Call Max in the morning and explain the situation, he'll listen to reason."

"You don't understand. He's not a reasonable man."

Violet shook her head. "Everyone is reasonable, dear, you just have to help them along. I'm sure Max will feel quite differently after he's had a good night's sleep."

"Max is an insomniac and I'd bet my left hand he doesn't get a good night's sleep. Tomorrow he'll be even angrier. I'll be back in London and married before you can say Jack Robinson."

"Poor baby," said Audrey. "What will you serve at the reception? Chicken or fish?"

"Pigs in a bloody blanket," said Cecil scowling.

"Bother it all," said Violet.

Cecil left the apartment feeling hopeless, and he was dead on about Max's insomnia. Max didn't sleep a wink. It was eleven thirty when he telephoned to scream at Cecil, and at four o'clock the next morning he was still wide awake. He had tried lying down briefly but he'd sweated through his sheets, and he'd been pacing back and forth in the darkness of his bedroom ever since.

Even for a man accustomed to long nights, this was gruesome. Max's face was flushed and his heart was pumping like the engine of a freight train. It was fury that kept him awake. Fury at the world, but also at himself. Max had always sworn never to play the game with men like Dick Burkus. Not because he didn't know how, but because it was beneath him. And yet his desire to get into the Avenue had tempted him to do it anyway. He'd pretended to be someone he wasn't, and if that wasn't humiliating enough to begin with, it was infinitely more humiliating to get caught in the act.

Max paced back and forth, reliving the dinner again and again in his head. He saw himself reaching for the tumbler and he saw the contempt in Dick's face when he called him a cunning bastard. Max couldn't bear it.

There was a package of chocolate pop tarts lying on top of the television and Max ripped it open and savagely bit into one. If he had owned a dog he would have kicked it. He felt a burning desire to yell at someone but he couldn't think who. Cecil was the only person that came to mind, but he'd already fired Cecil. "I'll unfire him," thought Max, "I'll unfire him just long enough to rip his head off, and then I'll fire him again."

"Telephone!" he cried in the darkness. "Get me a telephone!"

Max's cell phone was on the nightstand and he walked over to it while forming the opening lines of his diatribe in his head. He picked up the phone to dial Cecil's number, but he pulled up short because the phone rang of its own accord before he could punch the first number. Taken aback, Max peered out his window into the queer dim light of the New York streets. Who could be calling him at this hour?

Max looked at his caller ID but he didn't recognize the incoming number. He put the phone to his ear without speaking and waited for the voice on the other end of the line.

"Hello?"

It was a woman's voice, but not one Max recognized. It was a high-pitched warble with a distinctly English accent, and it sounded almost like a man pretending to be a woman, like a drag queen impersonating the Duchess of Marlborough.

"Hello?" said the voice.

"Who is this?" Max growled.

"I'm looking for Max Guberstein."

Max didn't answer.

"Mr. Guberstein? Is that you? Can you hear me?"

"I can hear you. Who are you and why are you calling me? Do you realize it's four o'clock in the morning?"

"Oh dear, I hope I didn't wake you."

"You didn't wake me," said Max in a friendlier tone. His

anger was subsiding. The simple act of holding a phone to his ear calmed his nerves, and he was curious to know who he was talking to.

"How did you get my number?"

"Am I speaking to Max Guberstein?"

"Yes."

"Good then, Cecil Biddle gave me your number. He told me you'd be awake, so I thought you wouldn't mind a call."

"Who are you?"

"It's Mrs. Penfield."

Max was losing his patience. He didn't know who was on the other end of the line but he knew it wasn't Trixie Penfield. An outrageous thought occurred to him. Was Cecil playing a prank on him? If so, he would pay for it dearly. There was menace in Max's voice:

"Cecil, is that you?"

"Calm down, Mr. Guberstein."

"Who is this!" Max bellowed.

"I've already told you," said the voice sharply. "I'm Penfield, Mrs. Violet Penfield."

"Violet?"

"That's right. We've not met but I believe you know my son. I'm Dante's mother."

After the events at Le Petit Chien, Max wasn't sure he wanted to talk to Dante's mother.

"Why are you calling me?"

"Well," said Violet, "I just flew in from London this week and I'm suffering a touch of jet lag. I woke up half an hour ago and wild horses couldn't drag me back to sleep. Cecil said you'd be up so I gave you a buzz. I have an idea I want to talk over with you. I thought we could meet for a cup of coffee. Or maybe you'd prefer a walk in the park."

"I don't take walks in the park," said Max.

"They're very good for you."

"What do you want to talk about?"

"I have a proposition. I heard about your trouble with Dick Burkus and I believe I can help iron things out."

"How?"

"Patience, darling. I'll tell you all about it when I see you. I'm told you live at the Pierre so why don't we meet in the dining room. I'm set to go as soon as I hang up. Is ten minutes enough for you?"

"Half an hour," said Max.

"Fifteen minutes. And don't be late."

By the time Max had showered and dressed, Violet was already in the dining room, seated at his customary table, pouring out two cups of coffee. Except for a lonely waiter, the place was deserted but Violet looked perfectly at home. Indeed, she looked so confident and self-assured that Max was somewhat undone by her presence.

"Violet Penfield?" he asked.

"Very astute. You must be Max. Sit down and have some coffee." Max didn't drink coffee but he accepted the cup without comment. "I've ordered us something to nibble on. Would you like a croissant?"

"Please," said Max.

"It's wonderful to be up at this hour, isn't it? You have the whole city to yourself. I drove down Fifth Avenue to get here and I felt I owned every block. Should I ask the waiter to bring you some eggs?"

"No thank you."

"Just as I thought," said Violet. "Cecil told me you were gruff, but I see you have excellent manners. Now, let's get down to brass tacks. I don't suppose you know where that phrase comes from?"

"From the upholstery trade."

"How clever of you to know that." Violet took a sip of coffee. "As I understand it, Max, you want to get into the Avenue Club."

Max hesitated in answering. He had his pride to consider and it was difficult for him to admit there was anything he wanted that he couldn't take at his leisure.

"You do want to get into the Avenue Club, don't you?"

"I do."

"I can't think why," said Violet. "They're a collection of use-less bores like any other, but I am not here to pass judgment, I'm here to help. Cecil told me about the apple juice incident, and don't look so grim, dear, it's quite funny when you see it in the right light. Dick tight as a priest and you just playing make believe. It's like that poker scene with Paul Newman from *The Sting*. More coffee?" Max shook his head and Violet topped up her own cup. "In any case, I imagine you gave Dick a good shock and he won't forgive it lightly. If you don't find a way to mend fences he'll certainly blackball you at the club. Fortunately, I have the solution to your troubles. All you have to do is take me up on a little proposal."

"What's that?"

"We'll get to it in a minute, Max. First I want you to give Cecil his job back, and you must promise to help him get this other job he's keen on. He said something about an interview at SouthEnd Pictures."

"What's your idea?"

"Not so fast, dear. Does Cecil get his job back?"

"Fine," said Max.

Violet gave him a tart smile.

"Do you have any idea," she said, "How expensive it is to open a restaurant in London? It's killing. I know because my friend Gascon is a chef. He's opening a restaurant and I've promised him the capital to get it started. But how does a girl raise the money? In my case, she sells a cottage on Long Island and you are the lucky man I've decided to sell it to."

"What do I want with a cottage on Long Island?"

"Hmpphhh, I thought you were smarter than that. I'll explain. My little cottage lies within a stone's throw of two much larger estates. One belongs to Puff Penfield, the other belongs to Dick Burkus, and both of them have been wanting to buy my cottage for years. As I understand it, you already have Puff's support at the Avenue but you still need to make Dick happy."

"I don't get it," said Max.

"It's quite simple. Here's what you do: you buy the cottage from me, and you arrange to sell it to Dick on condition you get elected to the club."

"What if Dick refuses?"

"He can't possibly refuse. Owning my cottage is his dream come true. It means his girlfriend has no excuse not to spend the summers with him, and it gives him the enormous plea-sure of poking a stick in Puff's eye. Puff has always thought he'd end up with the cottage, and Dick would love to snatch it away from him. He'd be in your debt forever."

"Interesting," said Max. "But what if Puff finds out? What if he discovers I'm selling the cottage to Dick? Won't he get upset?"

"Oh very," Violet replied. "But there's no reason for Puff to know. As far as he's concerned, the cottage belongs to me and I can sell it to whomever I wish. If Dick gets it, that's my business and you've got nothing to do with it."

"How much money are we talking about?"

"You needn't worry about that. The money doesn't matter because it won't cost you a penny. You buy it from me and you sell it to Dick straightaway after the election. You might even make a profit."

"I like it."

"Of course you do."

"Can we sign the papers today?"

"This afternoon if you like. There's just one more favor I need to ask of you."

"What?"

"We've already discussed Cecil's job, but this is something of interest only to me. My son says you're in the business of buying screenplays."

Max rolled his eyes. "You want me to buy your screenplay?"

"Not quite, I want you to commission me to write one. I haven't started it yet, but I have the idea in my head. It's based on a novel and I think it'll translate nicely to the movies."

"Hold on," said Max. "If it's from a novel that different. I'd have to work it out with the publisher before I agree to anything. Someone else probably owns the rights."

"I own the rights," said Violet.

"I've heard that before, but okay, let's say I believe you. How much do I pay for the commission?"

"Whatever you think is fair. Five percent of the gross?"

"Hah!" said Max instinctively.

"Three percent, then. Plus $60,000 up front."

"Writers don't get points. It's a flat fee. I'll give you $30,000."

"I thought you wanted to get into the Avenue."

"$50,000, but nothing up front. You get paid when you deliver the script."

"Thank you," said Violet patting Max's hand. "It looks like we're done. Talk to your lawyer and we can sort through the cottage paperwork later today. You'll need to call Dick to work out the club business, but don't forget about Cecil. I don't want him fretting any more than necessary. Are you sure you don't want a walk in the park?"

When Violet got home she went straight back to bed and when she next woke up it was eleven o'clock. Audrey had left to catch a train to New Haven where she was spending the night with a friend at Yale, and Dante was alone in the kitchen staring at a cup of tea.

"Congratulate me, darling," said Violet grandly.

"What for?"

"I've solved all our difficulties. I met with Mr. Guberstein this morning, and while the rest of you were sound asleep, we made an arrangement." There was a lot of colorful detail to be got through but eventually Violet explained the deal. "I sell the cottage to Max, he sells it to Dick, and Dick votes him into the club. It's brilliant!"

"What about Puff?" asked Dante.

"Puff can fry ice. He wants to sign on Monday, but if I put him off a few days, he won't know anything until after the elections and I'll tell him it was just business, that Dick had a higher bid. Isn't it glorious? Gascon gets his money, Max gets into the Avenue, and Cecil gets his job back with good prospects at SouthEnd Pictures."

Dante was delighted. "Good for you, mother. You've fixed it."

"I have."

"But I suppose that means there's nothing to keep you in New York," said Dante. "You know, I'll miss you. It's been lovely having you around."

"Don't worry Dante, there's no point in my rushing home. Gascon is so busy with his new restaurant, he hardly has time to speak to me. I think I might stay for a while."

"How long is a while?"

"A few months."

"How many months?"

"Three or four, it depends. The good thing is, if Audrey leaves for Iowa, you won't be all by yourself."

"I like being by myself," said Dante.

"I won't be in your way, darling. I'll be busy with my own affairs. I have work to do."

"What sort of work?"

Violet's eyes sparkled: "Max has commissioned me to write a screenplay!"

14

Having spoken to Max on Saturday afternoon, Dick Burkus woke up on Long Island Sunday morning feeling at peace with the world. Dick was a sensible man and he knew where his interests lay. He cared a great deal more about buying the cottage for Rebecca than he did about whether Max Guberstein drank scotch, and Dick was so pleased with the way things had come out that sitting up in bed, his thoughts turned to Puff and he felt a sudden urge to do something gracious. Puff had suffered enough, and he would suffer again when he found out he'd lost the cottage. It was time for the feud end and Dick was ready to take the first step. He went downstairs, ate two eggs on toast, and phoned his groundskeeper.

Meanwhile, across the way, Trixie Penfield was just starting her morning routine. Dry toast and tea in the kitchen, then back to her bedroom (Puff and Trixie had always kept separate bedrooms) for ten minutes of gentle stretching, followed by some breathing excercises, a shower, an exfoliating scrub, and finally a dose of the special revitalizing cream she ordered by the case from a shop in Paris.

Trixie gently patted the cream under her eyes and remembered her mother's old joke: Take care of your skin, said the starlet, and your bills will take of themselves. Trixie often thought of that joke as she did her toilette and it usually made her laugh, but she was in no mood for laughter today. She was worried about Puff. He hadn't been himself recently and Trixie took it as a bad sign. Of course, she'd always intended to tell him in the end, but she had wanted to do it on her own time. Now her hand was forced, the conversation could no longer be put off, and Trixie felt at sea, because goodness knows, she had no idea where to begin.

Worry not 'til worry's there, however, and since for the time being Puff was still fast asleep, Trixie got to work. Sitting down to her desk in the study, she placed a large pile of embossed stationary on one side and a typed list of sixty names on the other. Trixie still had to write her thank-you notes for the Balawala Elephant Park luncheon. The list of names told her who had showed up, and penciled in beside each name was a dollar figure reminding Trixie how much each person had donated.

Lala Von Furstenburg—$2,000

Trixie felt annoyed. Only six months ago she had paid $3,000 to attend Lala's dinner dance in support of the Whitney Museum and wasn't the survival of African wildlife worth more than a black and white photograph of Alan Ginsburg's penis? She bottled her irritation and wrote:

Dear Lala,
So lovely to see you at lunch. You're as beautiful as
ever and I thank you for your gift to the Balawala
Sanctuary. The elephants do too.
XXX OOO
Trixie P

Trixie crossed Lala off the list, but she had a long way yet to go. Sixty names meant sixty thank-you's and it wasn't a job that could be pawned off on Puff's secretary. To convey the right amount of gratitude, the notes had to be handwritten, and since Trixie's friends knew her handwriting, they had to be handwritten by her. It was tedious work but Trixie didn't object. In fact, she was happy for the distraction.

An hour later Trixie was signing her thank-you to Nana Johnson, for a healthy $6,000, when she was interrupted by the first sounds of Puff getting up. He was banging around in his bathroom, shaving presumably, and she put down her pen and listened to his movements. She heard him get dressed; she heard him go downstairs; she heard him ask Elena for a cup of coffee; she heard him carry his coffee to the dining room and start rustling the pages of the *New York Times*. Puff's habits were so unchanging that she knew them by heart, and she could almost see his lips moving as he argued with the editorials on the opinion page.

Trixie pictured her husband in his customary Sunday trousers, the arms of his oxford shirt folded neatly up above his wrist, and the thought of him brought a surge of affection rising into her chest. Trixie liked Puff. He wasn't the most charming man in the world but she had charm enough for two, and Puff had other merits. He was kind, reliable, and loyal, and he never made a fuss about money. No intelligent woman would ask for much else.

Trixie sighed quietly and continued writing her thank-you notes until she was shaken by the sound of a sharp crash coming from the dining room. It sounded as though Puff had banged his fist against the table and Trixie's concentration was broken. She couldn't get it back, and she started going over in her mind the horrible last few days they'd had together.

Never talkative under the best of circumstances, Puff had lately turned entirely mute. He wouldn't respond to simple questions; he would hardly even look at her; and when Trixie examined recent events in search of an explanation, she kept returning to the odd fact that Puff's ill humor coincided closely with a phone call she'd received from Max Guberstein the day after Cat's performance.

"The photograph," thought Trixie.

The subject was bound to come up sooner or later, but Trixie was nervous, and she was especially nervous because Puff's behavior suggested the worst. What she had to tell him would be difficult to swallow, but she had always harbored the hope that Puff would rise to the occasion. Trixie had hoped that his gentlemanly quality, his good manners, would trump whatever anger he might feel, but now she was no longer sure.

Trixie got up from her desk and went to look at herself in the mirror. What she saw in her reflection was a model wife. She was diligent, respectable and considerate; she was the mother of Puff's only child; and she had lovely skin. Thus reassured, Trixie took a deep breath and left the study to look for her husband.

She found him sitting outside on the terrace reading a book. His chair was facing the bay, and right away Trixie feared the worst. It meant that each time Puff looked up he would see the spite pole, and Puff only looked at the spite pole when he was contemplating the injustice of the world. Trixie coughed into her hand to get his attention.

"I need to speak to you," she said.

Puff didn't respond so she tried again.

"Are you alright?"

"I'm fine," said Puff frostily.

"What are you reading?"

"Don't ask stupid questions. You know very well what I'm reading."

Puff could be forgiven for his brusqueness because it was true that Trixie knew exactly what he was reading. She recognized the jacket cover from a distance. It was a copy of *Paisley Mischief*.

"What do you think?" asked Trixie. She knew the answer to this question too, but she needed something to say.

"I think it's despicable!"

Puff was not an emotional man, and he was more apt to seethe than yell, but he was yelling now and Trixie was surprised by his vehemence. She hadn't anticipated a fight about *Paisley Mischief* and she feared the conversation might run away from her.

"Then let's not talk about it," she said. "You shouldn't let yourself get worked up."

"What do you expect me to do? Do you expect me to laugh?"

"No, darling, I don't know. It doesn't matter. It's just a novel."

"Hush! Pay me the courtesy of shutting up for a moment and I'll give you a taste of your *just a novel*." Puff flipped back a few chapters to a page he had dog-eared and read out loud through clenched teeth:

> Reggie "Stuffy" Canbrook was a tall, blue eyed man who held himself ramrod straight at all times. In looks he resembled an embalmed corpse and his conversation wasn't much livelier. Stuffy lived by a script that had not been revised in thirty years and even in his most private moments his thoughts never strayed from convention. He was mesmerizingly dull and most especially on the subject of money. He'd lower his voice and let out a chuckle: "IBM is down forty-seven cents since last Tuesday, ha ha." That was Stuffy's idea of a joke, and his poor wife was bored rigid. She had come to dread the sight of him, but more than anything she dreaded the sound of his knock on her bedroom door at night. It was only once a month, but it was still one time too many. It was, she told her friends, like making love to a two-by-four. But at least two-by-fours don't drone on about real estate afterwards.

Puff shut the book and glared at his wife. Trixie was confused. "Why do you read it if it's just going to upset you?"

"Perhaps you should be answering that question," Puff said pointedly.

"But I have no idea."

Puff shivered. If he had to, he could live with a woman who felt a private contempt for him, but he could never live with someone who shouted her contempt from the roof tops, who mocked him openly, who published her insults in the pages of a popular book. When Puff read *Paisley Mischief* he wasn't just upset, he was bewildered. He thought of his marriage and he felt like he was watching the walls of a great city crumble.

"Do you think it's pleasant to be caricatured like that?"

"My darling, of course not. But I'm sure you're over-reacting and I can't see why you're asking me. I don't think you're the least bit like that man in the book. You're not boring and you're not a bad lover, I think you're an excellent lover, I've always thought so. You're the nicest man I know."

Trixie stepped forward and tried to put her hand on Puff's shoulder but he bristled and brushed it away.

"You can't whitewash over this. Words have meaning, and once they're written down they can't be unwritten. I'm not going to forget it. I won't say divorce, but there's no way we can continue as before."

"I don't understand you," said Trixie. "Divorce?"

"You betrayed me. You betrayed us. After twenty-five years you stabbed me in the back, and you did it in public. Your book has made me the laughing stock of everyone we know." He slammed his copy of *Paisley Mischief* onto the flagstones. "I can forgive a lot, but I cannot forgive this book."

For a moment Trixie was struck dumb. Then she realized what Puff was thinking, and her eyes went wide and she put her hand to her mouth. "You can't think I wrote that!"

"Indeed I can."

"I didn't!"

"Everyone else says you did."

"Who's everyone?"

"Dick Burkus," said Puff. "And Rebecca Holland."

"How would she know?"

"Because she's writing a magazine article about it. There's no use arguing, Rebecca got your name straight from the publisher."

"That's impossible."

"It is not impossible. It's plain as day. Rebecca met with the woman on Thursday."

"And the publisher said it was me?"

"She said the author's name was Penfield."

"There's more than one Penfield in the world."

"Are you suggesting I wrote the book?" asked Puff indignantly.

"No, but I promise you, I have absolutely nothing to do with that novel. You can search my desk if you like, search my e-mail. I didn't write it."

"Who did then?"

Puff sounded sullen. He wanted to believe his wife but he didn't know how. He stared at Trixie accusingly and she stared back. They were both racking their brains for an alternative solution.

"Dante?"

"Don't be ridiculous."

Trixie's eyes lit up. "What about Violet?"

"Hmmm," said Puff hopefully. "She is a Penfield."

"Of course! She's also an old friend of Dolly Smith's, and I know they talk on the phone. That's probably how she keeps up on all the gossip she put in the book. And goodness knows, she's never been bothered about offending anyone. Besides, isn't it odd that she arrives in New York just when there's such a uproar?"

"It makes sense," said Puff.

"It makes perfect sense."

"Damn that woman, pardon my French, but I bet you're right."

"Shouldn't we call her right now to make sure?"

"No," said Puff. He felt an enormous sense of relief. He was scheduled to see Violet tomorrow morning to sign the cottage papers, but he'd already decided he wasn't going to ask her about the book. All he wanted was to believe that Trixie was blameless, and at the first mention of Violet's name, he knew she was. Puff didn't care about anything else. His anger melted away and he looked up at Trixie rather sheepishly. "I'm sorry, my love. I've behaved very badly. I got carried away."

"Don't worry. It's funny really. I don't think I could write a novel to save my life."

"Certainly you could. I really am sorry though. I hope you'll forgive me."

"There's nothing to forgive."

"Here." Puff picked his copy of *Paisley Mischief* up off the terrace and handed it to Trixie. "Get rid of it for me. I don't want to look at it anymore."

Trixie took the book and went towards the house. She was about to go inside, but hesitated at the terrace door and turned back.

"Puff?" she said, but before she could make her mind up to keep talking, a cold wind blew onto the terrace and she felt a chill. Her arms broke out in goosebumps. "Never mind, I'd better go in."

Puff beckoned her to stay. "Wait Trixie, what is it?"

"Later, it's not important."

"If you've got something to tell me, you might as well tell me now. What is it?"

Trixie felt torn. She knew she had to speak to Puff eventually, but the unanticipated squabble about *Paisley Mischief* had drained her strength.

"Another time."

"Come back." Puff spoke without malice but with a surprising firmness. "What do you want to talk to me about?"

Trixie stared at her feet. "It's about Max Guberstein."

"Yes?"

"I got a phone call from him last week. He said you've got a photograph of his. You picked it up at the bar that night we went to see Cat's play. Max told me you held on to it because you wanted to make a copy for yourself."

"I did. I thought it was interesting from a historical perspective. The picture was taken outside our apartment building in the early sixties."

"I heard," said Trixie, "But I was wondering whether there wasn't some other reason you wanted to keep hold of it."

Puff nodded.

"That's what I thought. I've never known you to take an interest in architecture. I can't imagine why you'd care what our building looked like forty years ago."

"I don't care about the building."

"Do you have the picture on you?" asked Trixie. It was in Puff's wallet. "Do you mind if I look at it?"

Puff gave it to her and Trixie studied it for a while.

"Max looks the same as ever."

"He's fatter now," said Puff. "He looks more self-confident, too. Everyone changes as they get older."

"Do you like him?"

"Not really. Do I have to?"

"No, I don't much like him myself. I admire him in a lot of ways. He's very smart and driven, but he's too pushy for my taste. He always was, even as a child. I don't know where he got it from, because my father wasn't like that. My father was a gentle man, but Max always had a chip on his shoulder. He wanted to prove he was better than everyone else."

"Lots of people are like that. I knew boys in prep school who were the same," said Puff.

"Do you know why I introduced him to you? I had a sort of romantic notion that the two of you would become friends. I thought if you became friends to start out with, that would make it easier for me to explain the rest. Is that ridiculous?"

"It's not ridiculous, Trixie. It's not ridiculous to want me to be friends with your brother."

"My brother."

"Is that what you wanted to talk to me about?"

"Yes, it is."

"Well, there was no need to be so cautious. You could've told me sooner."

"I didn't know how," said Trixie. "It's been almost twenty-five years and the longer I waited the harder it got to tell you. That's why I asked Max to put himself up for the Avenue. I was hoping to do this bit by bit. I thought you'd have less trouble accepting it if he was in the club and you became friends."

"Don't take this badly," said Puff, "But he's not my type and I'm not his either. We're never going to become friends."

"I wonder if anyone becomes friends with Max. I don't even know that he has any." Trixie felt a tear in her eye. "I know all this must come as shock to you. I hope you're not angry."

"Sit down," said Puff. "I have something to confess to you as well. I may not be very bright but I'm not as stupid as some people think. I've known most of the story for a long time. Since before we were married. I always knew your maiden name wasn't Ashton."

"Why didn't you say something?"

"I didn't think it was my business."

"But you're my husband."

"If a woman wants to keep a secret, no one has the right to force it out of her."

"And you married me anyway?"

"Why not? It wasn't as though there was an army of girls beating down my door. You're the first woman I was ever close to and I fell in love. Nothing else mattered."

"What about your mother?" asked Trixie, "Didn't she object?"

"My mother was dying, if you remember. She could barely speak, let alone object. In any case, mother was full of odd theories about marriage. One of her ideas was that good families are in constant need of new blood. She liked to go on about cross pollination. I think she would've been pleased."

"But how did you find out? How did you know I wasn't Trixie Ashton?"

"It wasn't as complicated as you imagine. You used to have a bookcase in your office at the law firm. I was looking through it one day and I found a copy of *Great Expectations* that you must have kept from a high school English class. I opened it up and I saw you'd written your name on the inside cover. *Bea Guberstein*. I could tell it was your handwriting. It looked exactly the same as your other signature, *Trixie Ashton*. So I tracked down a copy of your high school year book. You told me you graduated in 1957, but there was no record of any Trixie Ashton graduating in 1957. There was only a Bea Guberstein, and she looked a lot like you."

Trixie sat down in the chair next to Puff.

"So you knew all along that Max was my brother?"

"I couldn't be certain, but I knew you shared the same last name and I had my suspicions. The photograph only confirmed them. You were a very pretty girl, you know. You looked good as a brunette."

Trixie studied the picture again. It was so far away, that day her parents dragged her and Max off to Manhattan for a family outing. Max had complained without ceasing all afternoon. He'd gotten into a shouting match with the waiter at the restaurant because his mashed potatoes were cold.

"I still remember it," said Trixie. "I remember posing under the awning and I remember wishing so hard that I lived in that building on Fifth Avenue."

"Now you do live there."

"Thanks to you."

"Can I ask you a question?" said Puff, "Why did you change your name?"

Trixie didn't answer.

"I'm just curious."

"Truly?" said Trixie. "You really don't know?"

"I guess I don't. I've never wanted to change my name."

"Oh Puff, that's because you're name is Wallace Penfield. Life is different when you're Bea Guberstein. At least it was thirty years ago. Or at least I thought it was. Maybe I was mistaken, I don't know, but after my parents died, I felt lost. I looked around and I saw how Max dealt with the world and I didn't want to be like him. I didn't want to spend the rest of my life fighting for respect. I wanted to start fresh, and that's what I did."

"I hope you don't regret it."

"No," said Trixie. "I don't. I wouldn't change a thing. I'm just glad to finally get it off my chest. In the last few years I've started to feel funny about it, as though some part of me were missing, the part I was hiding. I wanted to come out into the open."

For a brief moment Trixie thought of the young girl she once was and she was overcome by nostalgia. "You understand, don't you?"

"Of course I do," said Puff.

She kissed him lightly on the cheek and her bout of nostalgia was over. She was no longer Bea Guberstein, she was Mrs. Trixie Penfield, and she recovered herself.

"There's something I need you to do for me, Puff."

"What's that?"

"You have to make sure Max gets into the Avenue Club. He only put himself up as a favor to me and he didn't want to do it at first. But now the ball's rolling, and it's beyond my control. I can't pull him back anymore. Max has his heart set on becoming a member and he'll be furious if he gets turned down. You don't have to be Max's friend but you have to help him get into the club. I feel I'm responsible for him."

"You're not responsible for anyone but yourself."

"That's not what Max will think. His public image is at stake. If he doesn't get in, he'll never speak to me again."

"I'll do what I can," Puff replied. "But you have to understand, it's not entirely my decision. I've talked to the people on the admissions committee, but there's still Dick to contend with. There's nothing I can do about Dick. If he's against it, Max won't get into the club no matter what I say."

"Will you promise to try your best?"

"I will, but let's keep this between ourselves for the time being. There's no need for people to know Max is your brother and I'd prefer it doesn't become a topic of conversation right now. It would mean a lot of bothersome questions at the club."

Trixie stood up and patted her cheeks to bring the color back. "It's been quite a morning. I think I'll go finish writing my thank-you notes."

Trixie went inside and Puff leaned back in his chair. He crossed his arms behind his head and gazed out over the water. Suddenly he jumped to his feet as if poked by an electric cattle prod.

"My God!" he cried, "Look!"

Far in the distance Puff could see his cherished lighthouse. The giant American flag on top of the spite pole was waving no more. The top section of the spite pole had already been removed and the rest of it was slowly being dismantled by a small group of laborers who were packing it into a truck.

15

"She'll think of something. She has to."

That was the single thought that repeated in Dante's head as he walked down the long gray corridor on the fourth floor of the humanities building towards Audrey's office.

It was still Sunday morning and while it was unusual for teaching assistants to hold weekend office hours, the term was coming to a close and Audrey had been so inundated with requests for student conferences that she'd planned an early train back from Connecticut in order to make herself available. Which was very convenient for Dante because he desperately needed to talk to her, and with his mother in the apartment, it was impossible to talk privately at home.

At the end of the hallway Dante ran into a scruffy young woman slumped on the floor outside Audrey's office. She looked vaguely depressed and it wasn't hard to guess why. Taped upon the wall opposite was a notice announcing that the final papers for Professor Houghton's 19th Century Literature course were due on Monday. A cut-out paper arrow pointed to the table where the papers were meant to be handed in, and on the table were six wire "in" baskets, each one marked with the name of a different teaching assistant from Professor Houghton's course. A second notice reminded students, in big bold type, to "Put your paper in the right basket!" Some of the baskets were already half full, suggesting that a number of students had handed their papers in early, but presumably the scruffy girl on the floor was not among them.

The girl had greasy blonde hair and a pierced nose, but Dante found her very attractive.

"Are you waiting for Audrey?" he asked.

"You mean Miss Camp? Yeah, some guy just went in, but I'm next. I have to talk to her about this term paper. Do you know if she gives extensions?"

Dante didn't.

"I don't recognize you. What's your name?"

"Dante."

"I'm Lisa. Sorry, I'm terrible about faces. You're not in my section, are you?"

"No."

"Fuck," said Lisa, "I heard Miss Camp's really strict. If she doesn't give me an extension, I'm screwed. I haven't even started yet."

"What's the topic?"

"Pure bullshit."

Lisa pulled a xeroxed sheet from her bag and read it to Dante in a voice that was equal parts disdain and exasperation:

Using specific references to at least three novels on the syllabus, choose a single theme common to each novel and compare and contrast the various authors' handling of that theme.

"Compare and contrast," said Lisa. "I hate that phrase. You can't compare things without contrasting them. They're meant to be English teachers, don't they know it's redundant?"

"Me, I've never understood about themes," said Dante. "Most books are about human nature in the end, but you never get points for saying so. Why isn't human nature a theme?"

"I don't know, but I wish I had three thousand words on it by tomorrow." Lisa closed her eyes and groaned. "God, I hate this."

"Don't be upset."

"I can't help it. Even if I get an extension I won't have time to write anything. I'm a theater major and I'm performing every night next week. What am I supposed to do?"

Dante thought back to his own paper-handing-in days and he remembered feeling just as Lisa felt. Not much had changed since Professor Agnelli's Italian literature course. The same anxiety; the same incomprehensible paper topics; the same wire baskets.

"Can you keep a secret?" Dante asked.

"What kind of secret?"

Dante put his finger to his lips. "Sshhh. Keep your voice down. Normally I wouldn't recommend this sort of thing, but take a look at the table over there. Tell me what you see."

"I don't see anything. I see a bunch of wire baskets with a bunch of papers in them."

"What do you think the papers are about?"

"Same as I told you. Three novels, pick a theme, compare and contrast. So what?"

"Observe the number of baskets. There are six different

baskets with six different names on them, one basket for each teaching assistant."

"I don't get it," said Lisa.

"Let me demonstrate." Dante picked a paper out of the basket marked for Mr. Sangstrom. "Whoever wrote this essay is in Mr. Sangstrom's section and they're probably a good student because they finished early. Do you think Miss Camp is going to read it?"

"Why would she?"

"She won't. That's my point."

Lisa scrunched up her face as the implication sunk in.

"But I can't," she whispered.

"You can, it's easy. I did it once. I'm not proud of it, but it worked. The only person I hurt was myself and you'd be surprised how little that hurts. Isn't there a copier on this floor?"

"Outside the department secretary's office."

"Then take a paper, go make a copy, and put it back. After that all you have to do is re-type it."

"What if Miss Camp sees me?"

"I'll take care of that. I have to talk to her about something very important and by the time we're through, you'll be gone."

Lisa ran a hand through her greasy hair and thought it over. She looked at Dante, she looked at the wire baskets, and then she leapt to her feet, grapped a paper from Mr. Sangstrom's pile, and whisked off down the hall. A moment later Audrey's office door opened and the student inside came out, followed by Audrey herself.

"What are you doing here? Is something wrong?"

"Can I come in?" said Dante.

"Of course."

Dante shut the door behind him. "Mother met with Max Guberstein yesterday. He's buying the cottage."

"Why?"

"So he can sell it to Dick after the club elections."

Audrey pressed for further explanation. Having been away the night before, she was unaware of Violet's latest scheme and Dante had to fill in all the details. He tried hard not to minimize the positive aspects of the deal—Gascon gets his money, Max gets into the Avenue Club, Cecil gets his job back—but his main emphasis was on the one overwhelming negative: Max had commissioned Violet to write a screenplay and she intended to stay in New York to write it.

"She told me she might be here for months."

"Months?"

"Four at least."

Audrey twirled a lock of hair around her finger looking pensive, and Dante was pleased to see she understood the gravity of the situation.

"What am I going to do?" he asked pleadingly.

"I don't know, but we certainly can't have Violet in the apartment for four months. Besides, if anyone's going to sell a screenplay to Max, it should be you, not your mother." Audrey gently squeezed Dante's forearm. "I'm sorry, I shouldn't have let this happen. I should've been paying more attention to Violet. It's just that I've had so much teaching lately, and I'm still trying to finish my thesis."

Dante cheered up. Kind words from Audrey always melted

his heart, and it was enough to know that she was working on a problem for him to consider it half solved.

"That reminds me," he smiled, "Remember that book you were looking for, *The Senior Commoner*? I saw a copy of it in Tweedle's bookcase the night we put him to bed. I asked him at the club, and he'd be happy to lend it to you. He said to call any time and you can arrange to meet up. Here's his card."

"That's lovely, Dante. Thank you. But back to your mother, I'm going to have to give this some thought. Was there anyone else in the hall with you?"

"I was the last in line."

"Good. We can walk home together and discuss it on the way. Just give me a minute."

Audrey tidied her desk and put on her coat. She locked her office and stopping at the table with the wire baskets, she put all the papers from her basket into her briefcase. Then she did something unexpected. She put all the papers from Mr. Sangstrom's basket in her briefcase too.

"Those aren't yours," said Dante.

"They are now. That's why I've been so busy. Bill's got appendicitis and I agreed to take over his section."

Dante froze and covered his eyes with his hand.

"What is it?"

"Have I ever told about the 'A' I got in Professor Agnelli's Italian literature course?" Audrey waited for him to continue. "Yes, I think I have. Anyway, there was girl here when I arrived. Lisa, I think her name was. Greasy blonde hair and a nose ring. Does that ring a bell?"

"She's in my section."

"Well, I'm afraid I gave her some bad advice. I think Lisa may need an extension."

Understanding at once, Audrey looked for a moment like she was going to get very angry. But the intensity of Dante's regret was so evident that she took pity, and started giggling instead. Then she composed herself and putting on the sternest expression she could muster, she turned Dante round by the shoulders and administered three sharp slaps to his bum.

"I'll e-mail Lisa later. Let's go home."

"I picture that lovely blonde woman in the lead," crowed Violet sipping her tea the next morning, "And whatever happens, I won't let it run past a hundred minutes. It'll require cutting out some of the minor characters, but that shouldn't be too difficult. The key is to preserve the atmosphere of the novel. If you get the atmosphere right, you can take liberties with the plot."

While Violet talked about her screenplay, Dante ate a bowl of cereal and Lativia, the housekeeper, listened with an air of bemusement, shaking her head from time to time. Audrey came into the kitchen and poured herself a cup of coffee:

"What's the novel you're adapting? Not another Jane Austen, is it?"

"I'm afraid I can't tell you. It's confidential," Violet replied.

"Come on, mother. We'll find out sooner or later," said Dante.

Violet felt torn. Her sense of drama wanted to maintain the mystery, but her pride pulled in the other direction, and her pride won out. "You'll never guess, but it's *Paisley Mischief.*

I'm the anonymous author!" Violet waited for her applause, but Audrey and Dante were too astonished to speak. "Don't just sit there like beetles. You must have you read it. Did you like it?"

"Read it and liked it," said Audrey recovering.

"Me too," said Dante. "I thought it was great."

Beaming, Violet was curious to know how far her fame extended and she turned to ask if Lativia had read her book as well. Lativia had not.

"I'll tell you what though mother," said Dante, "You're better off staying anonymous until you get back to England. Lots of people are angry about it. Puff, for instance."

"Puff!" cried Violet. "Goodness, what time is it? Puff still thinks he's buying the cottage and he's coming over at ten o'clock to sign the papers. We've got to clear out. Lativia, darling, would you do me a favor?"

"What do you need?"

"There's a man coming this morning, my brother-in-law, and he wants to buy my cottage, but he can't and he mustn't find out."

"Why not?"

"Because I've already sold it to someone called Max. That's not important, darling. What's important is that you tell Puff I have to re-schedule. Tell him I had a dental emergency, and I'll call him next week. Can you do that?"

Lativia didn't deign to answer. "Go on. Get out of here so I can start cleaning."

Violet decided to take Dante to the MoMA and Audrey put them in a cab on 5th Avenue saying she had to go to work. But

Audrey didn't go to work. She watched the taxi until it was out of sight, then turned around and ran back to the apartment.

"Lativia, give me your apron."

"What's up, honey?"

"I don't have time to explain, just give me the apron. You start in the bedrooms and don't come out. I'll do the kitchen and living room."

Audrey hadn't even emptied the dishwasher before Puff arrived, Swiss prompt, at ten o'clock sharp. She answered the door in her apron and rubber gloves, and Puff, looking right through her, marched into the living room without waiting for an invitation.

"I'm looking for Mrs. Penfield," he announced to no one in particular.

Puff was nervous. Although he had no intention of discussing Violet's book with her, the knowledge that she had written it made him uncomfortable. He wanted to get the cottage papers signed and be on his way as quickly as possible.

"Hello! Violet!" he called.

"Mrs. Penfield's not in," said Audrey. "She had a dental emergency. She won't be back 'til this evening. Are you her brother-in-law?"

"Yes, I am. Who are you?"

"I'm Lativia, the housekeeper. Mrs. Penfield asked me to give you a message. It's about her cottage."

"That's right. She's selling it and I'm buying it."

"No, that wasn't the message. She told me to tell you the cottage has already been sold."

"That can't be."

"She said she sold it to a man named Max."

"Max Guberstein?" asked Puff incredulously.

"Something to do with a club. After Max gets into the club he's going to sell the cottage to Dick."

"Dick Burkus?"

"I don't know, sir."

Puff was stunned. It was inconceivable that Dick should get the cottage, and Puff now understood the dismantling of the spite pole in a new light. It wasn't a gesture of good will, it was a taunt. Dick was laughing at him, like a rich man who throws money at beggars on the street for the pleasure of watching them dive after it.

The bile rose in Puff's throat. Violet's cottage wasn't something he could afford to lose, and the fight wasn't over yet. If Max wanted to join the Avenue Club, Puff could have him blackballed just as well as anyone else, and it didn't matter whose brother he was.

"Young lady," he said, "I need to be absolutely clear. You say that Mrs. Penfield sold her cottage to Max, and Max intends to sell it to Dick. But Max hasn't sold it to Dick yet, has he?"

"That's right, sir."

"Thank you," said Puff. "You've been most helpful."

He reached for his wallet, handed Audrey a twenty dollar bill, and ran out of the apartment to hail a taxi that would take him to the Pierre hotel.

The events of the next six hours caused a small revolution in the affairs of almost everyone.

After an angry phone call, Puff and Dick were once again at

daggers drawn, and the spite pole, which had been removed on Sunday, was hurriedly re-installed late Monday afternoon.

Max Guberstein wasn't happy either. His brief meeting with Puff ended without resolution and he found himself lodged between Puff's rock and Dick's hard place. Both of them swore to exact revenge at the club elections unless Max coughed up title to the cottage, but since there was only one title and two men wanting it, Max was lost.

Naturally, Max needed someone to blame and Cecil bore the brunt. Max subjected him to an hour of raging abuse, then fired him again and blacklisted him for life. Under normal circumstances this might have been enough to restore Max's equilibrium, but he still had fury left over and the next person he went after was Violet. He cancelled her commission for the screenplay and put her next to Cecil on his blacklist. However since Violet wasn't in the movie business, the blacklist was an unsatisfactory punishment, and Max had to make the extra effort of calling her apartment every twenty minutes to leave rude messages on the answering machine.

Please leave a message at the beep: You bitch!
Please leave a message at the beep: You fucking bitch!
Please leave a message at the beep: You English cow!

Violet heard all Max's messages when she and Dante got back from the MoMA. No doubt Violet found them unsettling, but even more unsettling was the series of calls that came in about *Paisley Mischief*. The first of them was from Rebecca Holland, who, having spoken to Trixie, had discovered that Violet was the book's author:

Please leave a message at the beep: Hi. Rebecca Holland
calling for Violet Penfield. I'd like to interview you
about your novel. Why did you write it anonymously?
Any plans for a sequel? Please call.

Rebecca's message was harmless, but Trixie had such a large
network of friends that the news of Violet's authorship was
already widespread, and not everyone was so polite.

Please leave a message at the beep: Violet! It's Dolly Smith
here. I can imagine why you're not answering. This
book of yours shows very poor judgment. Cheap and
tawdry in my opinion. I had no idea you were taking
notes on our conversations. If I'd had any inkling I
never would've told you anything. You're a disgrace!

There was also a nasty message from Puff that took in both
the cottage and the book, and there were even messages from
people Violet had never heard of, like Pookie Wright and
Nana Johnson. Pookie wanted to know who Violet thought
she was; Nana went so far as to threaten legal action:

Please leave a message at the beep: My name is Nana
Johnson and I want you to know I intend to sue for
libel. My husband's firm will be sending you a letter!

Violet was at her wit's end. "Who's Nana Johnson?"

"A friend of Trixie's," Dante replied. "She thinks she's a
character in *Paisley Mischief*. She's the woman who tried to
seduce her daughter's boyfriend."

"But that's ridiculous! I wrote a novel! I don't know these
people, I made it up!" Dante shrugged and Violet stared

daggers at the answering machine. "You Americans are the most self-serious people in the world. I can't stand it."

For Violet, Nana Johnson was the nail in the coffin. She was fed up with New York and she had no desire to spend another minute being hounded by pissy socialites. Since the cottage was already sold, she decided on the spot to go home and give Gascon his money. She packed her bags, kissed Dante goodbye and took a taxi to Kennedy airport, where she bought a ticket at the ticket counter and caught the six o'clock flight back to London.

As soon as she left Dante's shoulders relaxed. He erased the messages on the answering machine, unplugged the telephone, and heaved a sigh of relief. He poured himself a glass of sherry and lay down on the sofa to marvel at the ways of fate.

A short while later there was a knock at the door and Cecil walked in.

"Mother's just gone back to London," said Dante. "Have a sherry with me."

"Cat piss. Where's Audrey?"

"On her way home from work. She should be back in a minute."

"I need to talk to that girl," said Cecil. "Actually, I wouldn't mind punching her in the face."

"What are you talking about?"

"Hasn't it occurred to you? Audrey was the one who blew up Max's chances at the club. It was Audrey who told Puff about the cottage."

"No, it was Lativia. Puff says so in the phone message. Audrey was at work, she wasn't even in the house."

"As far as you know, but think for a second. Puff comes running down to the Pierre and he knows everything about Max buying the cottage and selling it to Dick. Why would the maid tell him all that?"

"Because mother mentioned it at breakfast. Lativia just got confused."

"You're a ninny," said Cecil. "Don't you see? Audrey tells you she's going to work, but she goes back to the apartment instead. Puff barges in and she tells him she's the maid because she knows he won't recognize her and she doesn't want to get the blame from Violet. Audrey gave away the plan on purpose."

"I never thought of that," said Dante, hoping it was true.

Dante was still smiling to himself when Audrey walked through the front door. Cecil pounced:

"Why did you tell Puff about Max selling the cottage to Dick?"

"Calm down, movie man."

"Calm down? I just got blacklisted for life. Do you know what that means? I have to go back to London and I'll have to marry Penelope. Have you ever spent a week in the same house as Penelope?"

Audrey was unmoved. "You're a good friend Cecil, but the world doesn't revolve around you. I had Dante to consider as well. Violet was threatening to live here for the next four months."

"That's better than 'til death do us part."

"Besides," Audrey went on, "Do you think it's fair Violet gets her screenplay commissioned when Dante's been working on his movie for ages? If Max wants to buy a script he's can buy *The Darkness of Daisy's Back Passage*. Otherwise he can suck eggs."

"You're missing the point. If Max doesn't get into the Avenue, he's not buying anyone's screenplay. He's just going to ruin my life."

"Your life isn't ruined," said Audrey. "Have faith."

Cecil threw up his hands. "Faith in what?"

"In me."

"But there's no time left. The election is tomorrow night and Max is going to get blackballed. I'll never work in America again and next September I'll be walking down the aisle with Penelope in a white dress."

"You'd look good in a white dress," said Audrey.

"That's not funny."

"Then stop whining. You're not married yet and if you keep your fingers crossed maybe you never will be. Max can still get into the Avenue Club. Stranger things have happened."

"Unlikely," said Cecil with a sneer. His cell phone rang. It was Cat inviting him to dinner and he accepted. Cecil put on his coat. "I'm off to make hay while the sun shines. And next time I ask for your help, Dante, whack me on the head with a brick." He slammed the door on his way out.

"I like him," said Audrey, "But he can be very tiresome."

"Don't be too hard," Dante replied. "You've never met Penelope, you'd feel differently if you had. It's not surprising he's out of sorts."

"That's not what I meant. It's the defeatism I find annoying. It's just sexist arrogance. Cecil never wants to admit there are problems I can solve that he can't."

"But he's probably right in this case. Getting Max into the Avenue is a problem no one can solve."

"Why not?"

"I should think it's obvious. Puff and Dick are both going to blackball unless Max sells them the cottage and he can't sell it twice. It's not as though Max can sail through on the strength of his personal charm."

"We'll see," said Audrey. "I'm having a chat with Max tomorrow."

"About what?"

"I'd better not say."

"Not even a hint?"

"No."

16

Tuesday was election night and Dante's stomach was grumbling. He'd skipped lunch in anticipation of stuffing himself at the admissions committee dinner, but once inside the Package Room at the club he noticed the table wasn't laid.

"No dinner?" he whispered into Mr. Bullard's ear.

"Not on election nights."

"But I skipped lunch, I'm starving."

"Have some nuts."

Mr. Bullard pointed to a side table where a bar had been set up. Dante went to make himself a drink and scooped a large handful of mixed nuts out of a glass-lined silver bowl. John Newbury, the great seconder of motions, was at the bar putting ice into a tumbler.

"Watch out for the cashews," he said. "They'll give you indigestion."

"I never noticed."

"Perhaps they don't affect you in the same way. The cashews disagree with me. I don't know how many times I've asked the house committee to change the nut mix. I don't see why we can't have plain roasted peanuts."

Tweedle Barnes approached and Newbury moved away.

"Good evening, Dante."

"Hello Tweedle."

"I saw that Audrey friend of yours today. She stopped by to borrow the book you asked me about, *The Senior Commoner*."

"Oh good. I know she's been wanting a copy. It's nice of you to lend her yours."

"No trouble at all. She's a lovely girl and smart as a whip, too."

Wainwright broke in. "What's this? Tweedle's got a girl?" The Colonel poured himself a gin. "How's our Mr. Ball Bearer tonight? Ready to collect your bottle? It's life's blood to you, isn't it Tweedle? Pretty cushy appointment, if you ask me. Come to our meetings twice a year and walk home with a bottle of Glenlivet each time. No wonder you've been doing it for fifteen years. The only job you could ever keep!"

Wainwright winked and patted Tweedle affectionately on the shoulder. Tweedle, who had long since learned to put up with this sort of teasing, smiled gamely back at him. Dick Burkus rapped his knuckles on the dining table:

"Good evening gentlemen. I'm calling this meeting to order. Take your places and we can get started."

The members of the admissions committee arranged themselves in the same way as they had the week before. Dante, Newbury and Wainwright sat on one side of the table; Mr. Bullard, Jentsen and Sears sat on the other. Dick sat at the head of the table and Tweedle stood a few paces behind him, looking uncharacteristically grave. Tweedle's face was expressionless, he kept his head high in the air, and if he'd been holding a tray you might have thought he was a butler. This was Tweedle's customary pose on election nights. He stood at attention in order to indicate the seriousness of the business at hand.

"Welcome to the 132nd spring elections," Dick announced. The Avenue Club was 136 years old but there were four years during the World Wars when no elections were held. "Can I have a motion?"

"Motion to open the elections," barked Wainwright.

"Second the motion," said Newbury.

"Thanks," said Dick. "Now you're all familiar with the routine. As you know, I'm required to read the rules governing voting procedure before the election begins and if you just bear with me, I'll try to make it as painless as possible. Hand me the club rules, will you Tweedle?"

Tweedle stepped over to a bookcase and pulled out the rule book. It was a large volume bound in red leather with the club insignia embossed in gold on the spine. Dick flipped through it searching for the section on voting procedures. He cleared his throat and read aloud:

Club Voting Procedures — Chapter Fifteen, Section Six: Twice a year new members may be elected to the club. The President of the admissions committee will announce each candidate in turn. After a short discussion period, admissions committee members will place their vote. There is to be no bullying of committee members and each member must respect the decision of his fellows. Voting is to be done by secret ballot and members will vote by placing either a white or black marble in the ballot box. A white marble is a vote for admission, a black marble is a vote against. All committee members must vote on each candidate and all votes in favor of admission must be unanimous. Committee members may not abstain.

After each candidate has been voted on, the Ball Bearer will carry the ballot box to the President's office. The President must examine the contents of the box in the presence of the Vice-President and the Secretary. The Secretary may thereupon announce the results of the election and the President will inform each candidate of the club's decision.

"Blah, blah, blah," said Dick.

He closed the rule book and pushed it away, but Tweedle pushed it back to him saying, "I think you forgot something."

Apparently this was a joke, because a number of the committee members laughed.

"Just testing you, Tweedle," said Dick. He re-opened the rule book and read another short passage:

Club Voting Procedures — Chapter Fifteen, Section Seven: At the close of the elections, the Ball Bearer is entitled to a fifth of whiskey from a distillery of his choice. The bottle will be paid for by the club and the Ball Bearer need not sign a chit.

"Thank you," said Tweedle decorously. He put the rule book back in the bookcase.

"Any questions?" asked Dick. "No? Good. Remember, we want to keep things moving along. This is not the time to fight old battles. If you have to comment, keep it brief. Okay, let's get started. The first candidate is Charlie Blister, Danny Blister's son. Can I get a motion to vote?"

"Motion," said Wainwright.

"Second," said Newbury.

"Motion to vote is seconded." Dick turned to Dante. "Off your knees, Dante. We do this in order of age, youngest to oldest. You'll have to get us going."

"I've never done this before. What do I do?"

"Pretty simple," said Dick. He pointed to the far end of the room where a Chinese screen had been set up. "The ballot box is behind the screen and there's a bowl of marbles next to it. All you have to do is pick a marble and put it in the box."

Dante got up and went behind the screen. Just as Dick said, there was a mahogany box about the size of a toaster oven, placed next to a large glass bowl filled with black and white marbles. Dante studied the box for a while wondering how the marbles got in. He tried lifting the lid but it was locked; he looked for a drawer to pull out but there wasn't any; at last he found a small hole drilled through the side of the box that was just big enough to fit a marble. Dante bent over and peeked inside but it was too dark to see anything. He reached for the bowl of marbles.

White or black?

Dante was suddenly struck by a strange sense of his own importance. Everyone at the club expected Charlie Blister to get elected as a matter of course, but all Dante need do was drop a black marble through the side of the box and that expectation would be turned on its head. Dante took a black marble and weighed it in his hand. It wasn't that he disliked

Old Money

Charlie Blister, he was simply curious. He'd never had the power to decide someone else's future before and he wanted to know what it felt like.

"What the hell!"

Dick's voice came booming from the other side of the Chinese screen and Dante was brought back to his senses. He put the black marble back in the bowl and picked up a white one instead. He popped it quickly into the ballot box and stepped out from behind the screen.

"You must have been growing a beard back there," said Dick.

"Sorry, I had trouble finding the hole."

"Don't tell your girlfriend that. Alright Jentsen, come on, you're next."

As the first round of voting proceeded, Dante felt a growing tension. He'd meant to put a white marble in the box, but it was so easy to get confused and now he wasn't sure. He might have grabbed a black marble by mistake. And what if Charlie Blister didn't get elected? Everyone in the room would remember the time Dante took casting his vote and they'd blame him for the blackball.

The last man to vote was Mr. Sears, the oldest member of the admissions committee, and when he stepped out from behind the screen, he carried the ballot box with him. Dante heard the marbles rolling around inside it, and he crossed his fingers that they were all white. Sears handed the box to Tweedle, who left to take it up to the President's office.

"Tweedle!" said Puff, happily ensconced behind a giant desk. "Who's the first candidate tonight?"

"Charlie Blister."

"Very good, give me the ballot box."

Puff took the box and unlocked it with a small key he kept in his desk drawer. He opened the top and asked the Vice-President and the Secretary to look inside. After examining the contents it was up to the Secretary to make the official announcement:

"Seven members of the admissions committee and seven white marbles. Charlie Blister is a member of the Avenue Club."

Puff took out all the marbles, re-locked the box, and gave it back to Tweedle, who returned to the Package Room and put it back behind the Chinese screen.

The next two rounds of voting passed quickly. Mark Sawyer and Billy Simington were each elected to the club without incident, but the fourth candidate of the night provided the committee with its first taste of controversy. The candidate was Darius Vajpayee, the Indian son-in-law of Hammy Thomas, and Dick and Wainwright came out firmly against him. Jentsen, on the other hand, was strongly in favor, and he insisted on making an impassioned speech on Vajpayee's behalf. Jentsen argued that the Indians were in New York to stay and that the club had to adapt, but it was a lost cause in the end. Darius was not only turned down, he received three black balls, meaning that he was prohibited from becoming a candidate for membership ever again.

Finally it came down to Max Guberstein. He was the last man up for election and he generated by far the most debate. Sears and Jentsen said they were in favor, Newbury chose not express an opinion, and Wainwright, at great length, explained why he was on the fence. After a brief lull, Dick took the opportunity to speak:

"Before we motion to vote, I'd like to say a few words myself. As you know, I had dinner with Max a few days ago and I promised the committee a report." Dante braced himself for a firestorm, but Dick remained calm. His tone was mild, his words were generous. "I found Max to be excellent company. He's a smart man and a good man, and after our dinner together I can honestly say I'd be pleased to have him as a fellow member. I think he'd make a good addition to the club."

This little speech caught Dante so off guard that one of the nuts he was eating got stuck in his throat, prompting a short fit of coughing.

"It's the cashews," Newbury murmured.

"Can I get a motion?" asked Dick.

"Hold on a minute," said Mr. Bullard. "I'd like to add a few comments. We've heard what Dick has to say, but I want the committee to understand that I'm in perfect agreement with him. I think Max would make an excellent addition to the club, and I'm not just speaking for myself, I'm speaking for Puff Penfield as well. Puff has asked me to advise the committee that he considers Max a good friend and every bit deserving of membership."

"Well, well," spluttered Wainwright. "I must admit, I had my doubts about Guberstein. But if Dick and Puff are squarely behind him, I see no reason not to go along with their judgment. I'm for it."

"Anyone else?" asked Dick. The room was silent. "Motion?"

"Motion to vote," said Sears.

"I second the motion," said Newbury.

Dante's head was spinning. Audrey, he said to himself, must be a genius. How did she do it? Dick and Puff had stood up for Max's election. What had happened to change their minds?

Were Dante less naïve, he would have realized that the answer to this question had nothing to do with Audrey. It had to do with Violet's cottage. Dick and Puff were posturing. Dick intended to blackball Max, and Mr. Bullard, on Puff's instructions, intended to do the same. The kind words were entirely insincere. They were only spoken on the assumption that whatever was said at the meeting would eventually get back to Max, and since both Dick and Puff wanted to buy the cottage, each of them was hoping to blame the other when Max got rejected at the club.

Still puzzled, Dante rose from his chair and went behind the Chinese screen to cast his vote. He put a white marble in the ballot box, returned to his seat, and the rest of the committee members voted in turn. Sears voted last and afterwards handed the box to Tweedle, who carried it away.

Up in the President's office, with the elections almost over, the club Secretary was now smoking a cigar while Puff and the Vice-President were chatting amiably about the evils of trade unionism. Tweedle interrupted them.

"The ballot for Max Guberstein."

"Thank you," said Puff. "If I'm not mistaken this is the last of the night."

"It is."

"Very good then, Mr. Ball Bearer. Here's to a job well done."

Puff reached down behind his desk and handed Tweedle a

bottle of whiskey. Tweedle opened it and poured himself two fingers. He took a sip and cleared his throat.

"If you don't mind," said Tweedle, "I have an announcement of sorts. This will be the last time I drink from the Ball Bearer's bottle. I'm resigning."

"Tweedle!" Puff exclaimed.

"Why would you do that?" asked the Secretary.

"Because I'm resigning from the club. I'm giving up my membership."

"You can't," said Puff. "You're an institution."

"The Avenue Club is the institution. I'm just an old man."

"But what are you going to do with yourself?"

"I going to look for a place outside the city," said Tweedle. "I've lived in Manhattan for decades and I'm tired of it. I want a change of scenery."

"Old dogs and new tricks, Tweedle," said the Secretary wagging his finger.

"I hope that's not the case."

"Of course it won't be," said Puff gently. "We wish you the best of luck. We'll miss you."

"Thanks. Now can I offer anyone a drink? You might as well accept because I'm not taking the bottle home."

"Why not?"

"I'm giving up the habit."

"Give up whiskey? Are you sure you're alright?" asked Puff.

"Never better," Tweedle replied.

Puff, the Vice-President and the Secretary stared at Tweedle in disbelief. Then they all stood up to shake his hand. Tweedle gave them each a drink and made a toast to the club.

"Right," said Puff. "Back to business. The ballot box for Max Guberstein."

He unlocked the top with his little key and casually flipped open the lid without even bothering to look inside.

"Max Guberstein has been blackballed," said Puff. He turned to the club Secretary. "Do me a favor. Would you mind calling Max in my place? I have a certain relationship with him and I'd rather not deliver the bad news myself."

"I'm afraid you've gotten ahead of yourself," said the Secretary.

"It's a simple telephone call," said Puff.

"No, wait," said the Vice-President peering closely into the ballot box and counting the marbles himself. "Yes, they're all there. Seven members of the admissions committee and seven white marbles."

"What?" cried Puff.

"It's seven white marbles," said the Secretary, confirming the count. "Max Guberstein is a member of the Avenue Club."

Puff snatched the box towards himself and stared down into it. The Secretary was right. Seven white marbles. Puff felt like he'd been punched in the stomach.

17

A fortnight later, as waiters in tuxedos scurried back and forth carrying silver trays full of hors d'oeuvres, Max was nursing a club soda in the Pratt Room at the Avenue's semi-annual dinner for new members. The whole club was there, but Max stood by himself. A few yards away, he could hear Charlie Blister and his father talking excitedly with four other men about the results of the most recent court tennis tournament, but there wasn't a single nerve in Max's body that felt any desire to join them.

Looking around, Max noticed Jentsen weaving through the crowd towards him and he gritted his teeth.

"Max!" said Jentsen thrusting out his hand for a shake, "Congratulations, it's good to have you on board. We need more men like you in the club."

"Thank you," said Max barely managing to sound polite. Jentsen's bleeding heart had been useful during the elections but Max hated his bumptious cheerfulness and he didn't much like the phrase "men like you" either. What sort of man did Jentsen think he was?

"I mean people with a social conscience," said Jentsen. "People who want to give back. I heard about your generous gift to the Balawala Elephant Park and I was very impressed. As it happens, I have a special interest in species conservation myself."

Max knew where Jentsen was headed and gave him a cold stare, but Jentsen was undeterred.

"Education is the most important thing, we have to get young people involved. That's why I'm active with the Independent Schools Wildlife Initiative. It's a organization that takes exotic animals around to elite boarding schools all over New England, and I was hoping you might want to join me on the board of directors."

Max laughed out loud and Jentsen stiffened.

"It's a serious matter, Max. We're teaching the concept of biodiversity to our next generation of leaders. We need your help."

"Well, you're not getting it. I'm a movie producer, not a zoo keeper."

On the far side of the Pratt Room, Dick Burkus and Mr. Bullard were talking quietly together. It was the first time they'd had a chance to speak since the election. Mr. Bullard glanced over at Max across the room, then took a sip of his bullshot, a club specialty made from vodka, bitters, and beef consommé: "I'll say this Dick, the new membership lists came as something of a shock."

"You're telling me."

Dick chewed his lip. It was a riddle he couldn't figure out. In the days since the election Dick had asked himself countless times how he could've gotten so confused, how he could've put a white marble in the ballot box instead of a black one. Of course it was a simple mistake in a way, but in all his years on the admissions committee, it had never happened to him before, and looking back, he still couldn't believe he'd done it. He could still see the black marble on his fingertips, and he could've sworn he put it in the box.

"One thing I don't understand," said Dick.

"What's that?" asked Mr. Bullard.

"This is just between us. I know you and Puff are close, and I'm not asking you to tell me anything you shouldn't. But I've known Puff for ages and I'd bet my life he didn't want Max to get into the club. So how come you spoke up for Max at the election? How come Puff didn't ask you to blackball him?"

"I suppose I could ask you the same thing," said Mr. Bullard cautiously.

"Fair enough, but just tell me this. Didn't you mean to blackball him? Did you think you had?"

Mr. Bullard shrugged without answering. He was too discreet to discuss it with Dick, but Mr. Bullard was also deeply puzzled by the election results. Because the fact was, Puff had told him to blackball Max. And Mr. Bullard had meant to do so. Indeed, he thought he had. Like Dick, he could picture himself holding a black marble in his hand, and he felt almost certain he had dropped it into the ballot box.

"Well it's bullshit if you ask me," said Dick. He stared hard into Mr. Bullard's eyes for a moment, trying to see behind the veil, but to no avail.

"It's no use crying over spilt milk, Dick. What's done is done and Max is here to stay. The only way to we can get rid of him now is if he stops paying his dues, so we might as well make the best of it. I'm going over to say hello. Do you want to come?"

"No thanks, you go ahead."

As Mr. Bullard wended his way slowly across the Pratt Room, Max found himself talking to Dante about *The Darkness of Daisy's Back Passage*.

"It's not worthless," said Max kindly. "But I'd have to hire someone to fix it. No one could use what you've got so far, not even the title. Are you kidding me?"

"You can change the title," said Dante.

"I know that, young man. I bought the option. I can change whatever I want."

"What else would you change?"

"The ending," said Max. "The ending doesn't work."

In Dante's latest version, he'd decided that he liked Daisy too much to convict her of murder, so he turned the story around to make her innocent. In the new version, Daisy's husband dies of an ordinary heart attack and in the end Caleb Astor realizes as much and asks Daisy to marry him. Max thought this was outrageous.

"You can't write a murder mystery and then tell me there's no murder. That's a breach of contract. When you write for the movies you have to be fair to the audience."

Mr. Bullard stepped forward to interrupt: "So that screenplay of yours finally worked out, Dante? Good for you."

"Hi, Mr. Bullard."

Old Money

"Hello. And hello to you Max. Let me shake your hand. Welcome to the Avenue Club."

The new members' dinner proceeded far into the night. Cocktails led to dinner, which led to wine and coffee and brandy. Speech followed upon speech and toast followed upon toast. With the exception of Max everyone got fairly drunk. Poor Charlie Blister passed out cold in the billiards room at two o'clock in the morning, but by that time, Dante had long since gone to bed.

Dante went home early because he had work to do the next day. He and Audrey had agreed to drive a moving van out to Long Island, and by noon the rental was double parked on 81st Street and they were busy carrying furniture and boxes down the dirty staircase from Tweedle's tiny apartment. It took less than an hour to pack everything up, and then they drove south down Second Avenue, through the Midtown Tunnel, and out onto the Long Island Expressway.

When they arrived at Violet's cottage, Tweedle was standing in the driveway to greet them.

"Did you sleep well?" Dante asked.

"Like a dream. My first night in the cottage and I felt more at home than I have in forty years. I don't know how to thank you."

"Don't thank me," said Dante, "It was Audrey's idea."

Tweedle kissed her lightly on the cheek, then he stood back and studied her with open admiration. Dante smiled. There was no taking it away, she was a very resourceful girl.

"Stop it," said Audrey blushing.

Dante and Audrey unloaded the moving van and afterwards Tweedle made coffee in the kitchen while talking through his plans for a vegetable garden. If he got started right away he might still have tomatoes in August.

"Milk and sugar for either of you?" asked Tweedle, passing the mugs around. He reached into a cabinet above the sink and poured a large splash whiskey into his own cup. "If you don't mind, I like mine warmed up."

"I thought you were giving that up," said Audrey.

"Oh I was, I was. But I couldn't last past the third day. No will power. And anyway, it threw my system out of whack. Terrible stomach aches. So, I thought, who needs it? Change doesn't have to be radical. Moving here is a big enough step for now."

They all sat in silence for a while drinking their coffee.

In the middle of the kitchen table was a small glass bowl with two black marbles in it. Dante picked them up and started playing with them absentmindedly.

"Those belong to Max," said Tweedle. "I saved them for good luck."

"How did you open the ballot box? Did you have to pick the lock?" asked Dante.

"Oh no, it was much simpler than that. I just borrowed the key from Puff's desk in the afternoon and made a copy of it."

"Do you think Puff knows?"

"Perhaps, but I doubt he'd want to make a fuss, and in any case, I don't care. I'm too old to bother."

"And Max didn't mind about leasing the cottage? Is he making you pay rent?"

"No, Audrey took care of that," said Tweedle, raising his mug to her.

"My pleasure," said Audrey. She looked at her watch. "We should probably be going. We have to get back to the city to meet the new head of SouthEnd Pictures."

Cecil was flying to Los Angeles tomorrow but he had insisted on taking Audrey and Dante out for a celebration dinner before he left.

"Visit again soon," said Tweedle.

"We will," Audrey replied.

She and Dante got in the van and drove west back to Manhattan along the expressway. They dropped off the rental van on 96th Street and walked quietly home through the lengthening shadows of late afternoon.

"What's wrong?" said Audrey.

"Nothing's wrong."

"I don't believe you, Dante. You haven't said a word since we left Tweedle's. There's something in your head, I can tell. What is it?"

Dante stopped walking and stared down at the sidewalk. He felt too shy to look Audrey directly in the face. He tried to collect his thoughts but he had butterflies in his tummy and when he started to speak he had to make a great effort to prevent his voice from cracking.

"Are you really going to move to Iowa?" he asked.

"I haven't decided yet."

"But do you want to? I mean, don't you like it in New York anymore?"

"Don't be silly, Dante. Of course, I like it in New York. I love it here. But they're offering me a lot more money to study in Iowa. It doesn't make sense to turn them down."

"Why not?"

"Because I need to get my doctorate, and I can't afford it otherwise."

"What if you could though?" asked Dante. "What if you could afford to get your degree in New York?"

"But I can't."

Dante was silent for a moment.

"You know I got something in the mail from GoldStream Pictures last week. It was a check from Max, the option money for my screenplay. Do you know how much it was for? $50,000. That's roughly the same as the difference between what they'd give you in Iowa and what you'd get here."

Audrey nodded.

"I never properly earned the money," Dante continued. "You did. If it weren't for you, Max never would have bought my screenplay in the first place, so really the money should be yours. And if you took it, you could stay in New York."

"I can't take that money," said Audrey.

"But you must, you have to. I'd hate it if you left. I'd fall apart in an instant."

"You would not fall apart, you'd be fine."

"I'd miss you."

"I'd miss you, too."

Dante bowed his head and Audrey felt suddenly overcome by tenderness. She didn't cry but she reached out to touch Dante's hand.

"Won't you please take the money?" he said.

Old Money

Audrey wondered what to do. Her pride tempted her to refuse but when she looked in Dante's eyes she saw that pride is sometimes foolish. Audrey didn't want to move to Iowa any more than Dante wanted her to.

"I'm very happy where I am," she said.

"So you'll you take the money?"

Audrey said she would.

The Aways
Astoria, 2012

Made in the USA
Charleston, SC
19 June 2013